SEVEN SMALL INVENTIONS THAT CHANGED THE WORLD

ROMA AGRAWAL   JISU CHOI

Laurence King

To the curious kids all around the world, and to the grown-ups who nurture that curiosity – R.A.

Thanks to Roma for offering me this challenge and opportunity, Ella, my running mate for a year, and my friends who firmly told me 'you're going to make something great' – J.C.

LAURENCE KING

LAURENCE KING
First published in the United States in 2024
by Laurence King

Text copyright © Roma the Engineer Ltd 2024
Illustrations copyright © Jisu Choi 2024

All rights reserved.

HB ISBN: 978-1-510-23076-7
PB ISBN: 978-1-510-23078-1

10 9 8 7 6 5 4 3 2 1

Kevlar ® is a registered trade mark of DuPont Safety & Construction, Inc. Slinky ® is a registered trade mark of Poof, Slinky LLC.

Printed in China

FSC MIX Paper | Supporting responsible forestry FSC® C104740

Laurence King
An imprint of
Hachette Children's Group
Part of Hodder and Stoughton
Carmelite House
50 Victoria Embankment
London EC4Y 0DZ

An Hachette UK Company
www.hachette.co.uk
www.hachettechildrens.co.uk
www.laurenceking.com

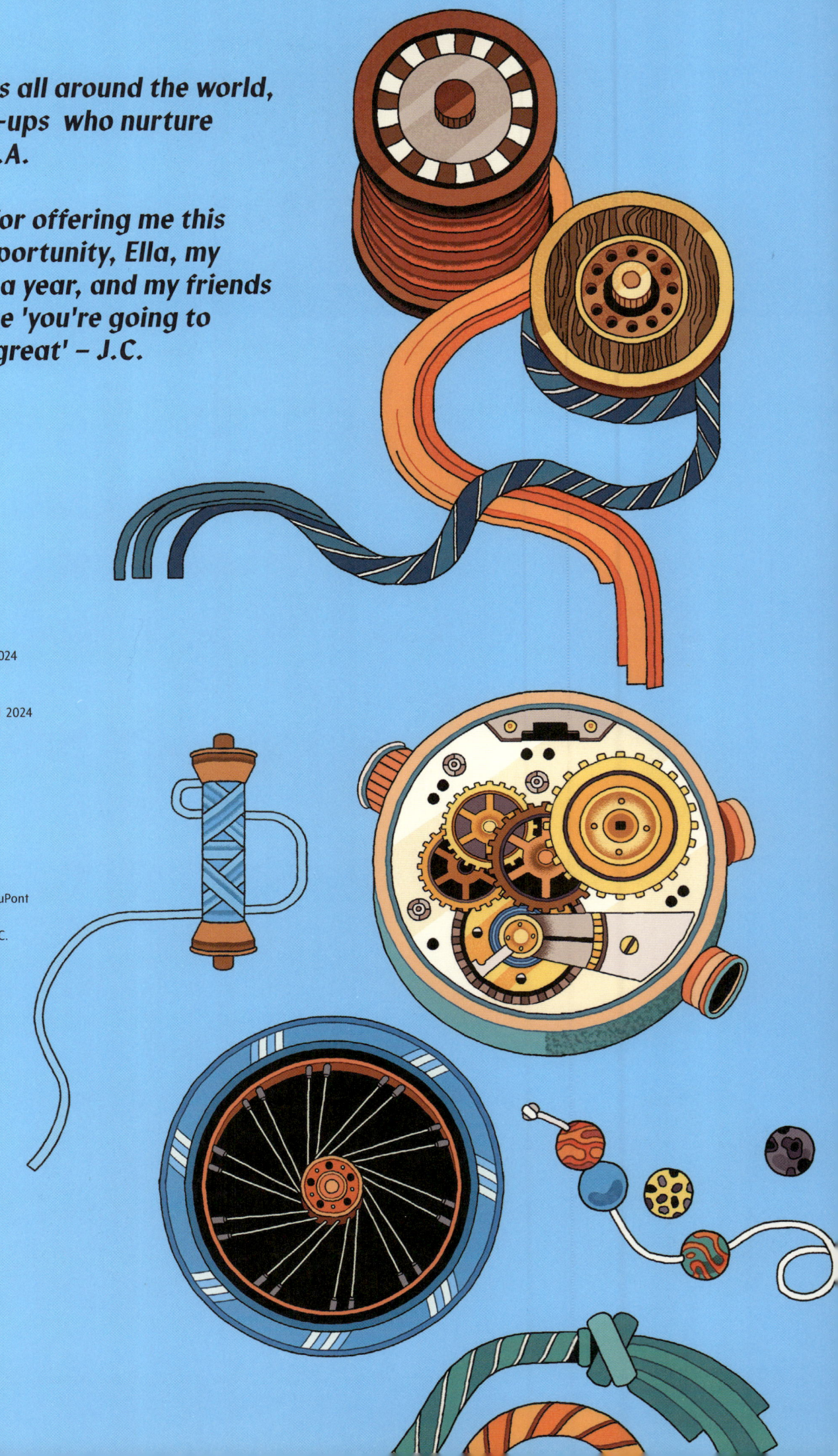

CONTENTS

PAGE 4
SMALL YET MIGHTY

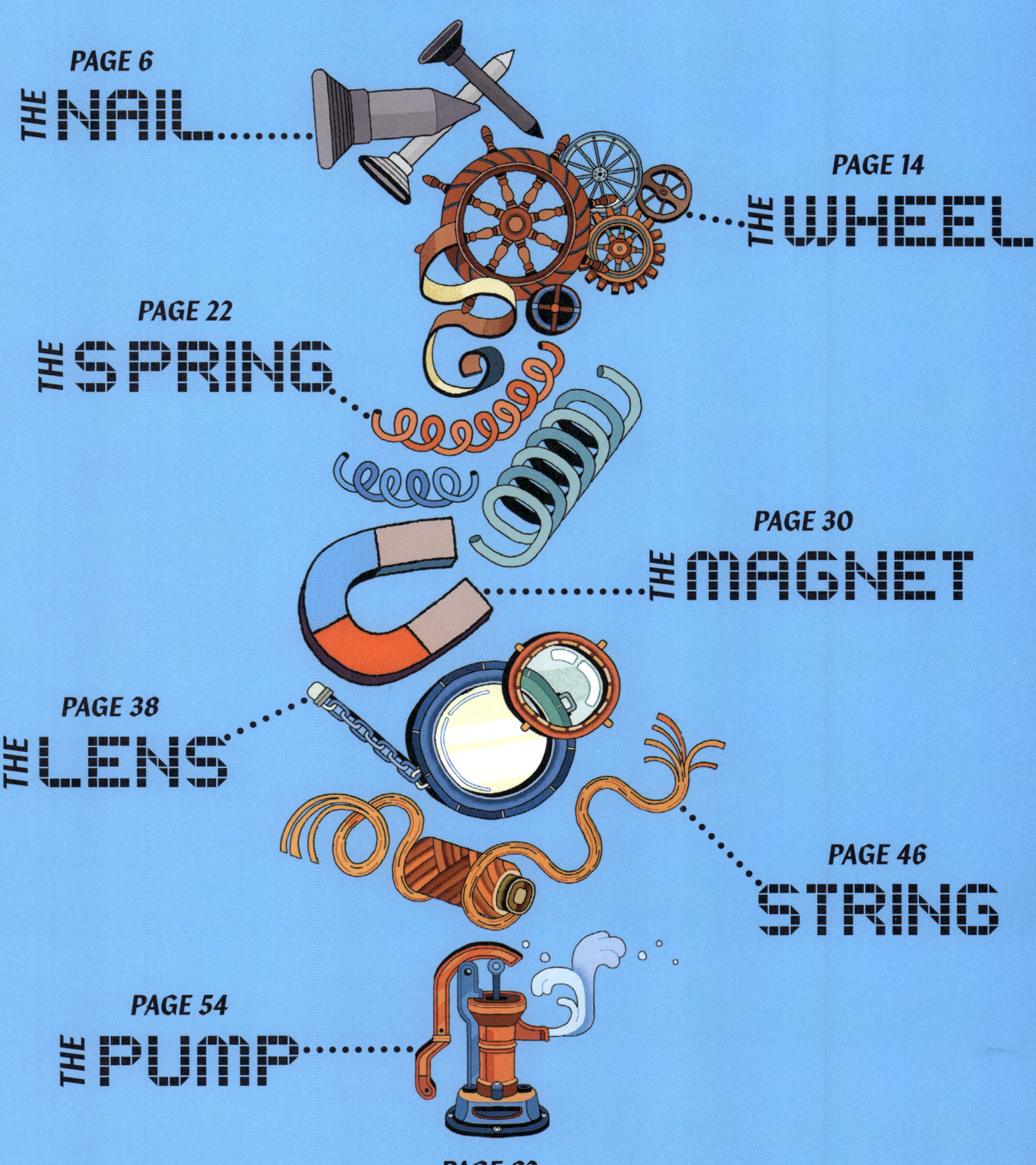

PAGE 6
THE NAIL

PAGE 14
THE WHEEL

PAGE 22
THE SPRING

PAGE 30
THE MAGNET

PAGE 38
THE LENS

PAGE 46
STRING

PAGE 54
THE PUMP

PAGE 62
WHAT WILL YOU INVENT?

SMALL YET MIGHTY

One of my earliest memories, aged five, was cracking open my crayons to 'discover' what was inside them. Now, before you do this, be warned – the results aren't all that exciting. Crayons look the same on the inside as the outside! So it wasn't until I was older that I discovered crayons are actually *really* interesting – they are a mixture of a type of wax and chemicals (called pigments) that give them color. The wax, called paraffin, is made from petroleum, which is pumped *all the way* from deep beneath the earth's surface.

A few years later, when I was around seven, I decided I might have more luck with opening up a ballpoint pen. These are the things I found . . .

a cartridge with a ball at the end . . .

a tiny spring . . .

and some pieces of plastic that were screwed together.

Three small things that came together to make something brilliant.

So, I started asking questions about the small things – who invented the spring and when? How does the ink travel through the cartridge to the little ball at the tip? And how was this ball made?

As I grew older, I dismantled *more* things, and looked for the answers to my questions. I realized that *all* the stuff around us is made up from smaller, really important things; things that have awesome histories and interesting science of their own. I learned that the ball in the pen was a more sophisticated version of a flat disk or a wheel. I learned that the wheel was not invented for transport, though we might think it was. I learned that the coiled metal springs are actually a very recent invention and before that, arc-shaped springs were used, like the bow (and arrow) – and that a bow *is* a type of spring! And I learned that screws, now made in bulk and cheap to buy, were once expensive and difficult to make.

Although the technology and engineering that surrounds us seems incredibly complex, every invention is made from a series of *smaller* building blocks – amazing inventions that have tremendous tales of their own, like these . . .

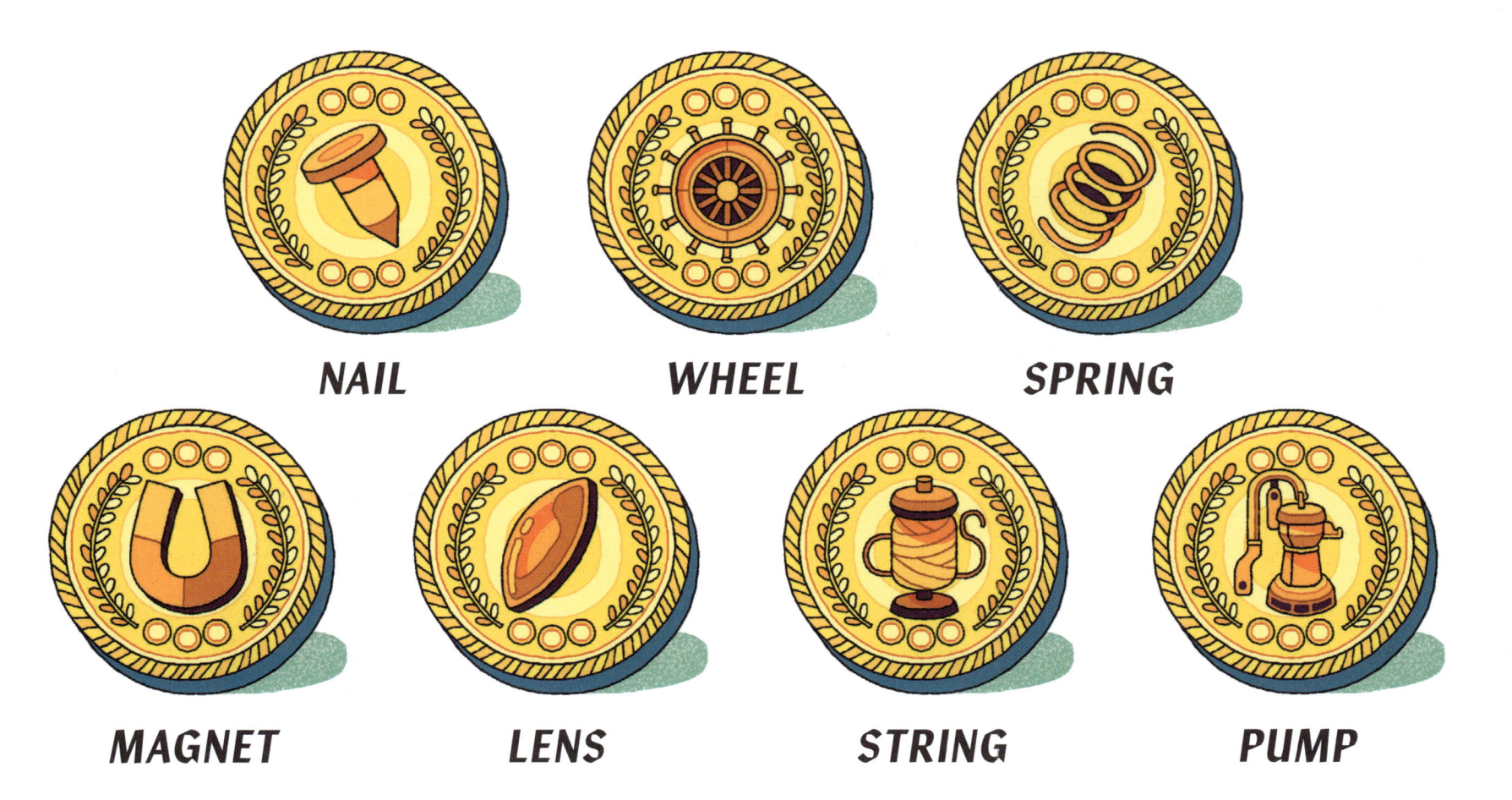

NAIL **WHEEL** **SPRING**

MAGNET **LENS** **STRING** **PUMP**

Each of these seven inventions, although often hidden, is an extraordinary example of engineering. And ALL of these inventions have fascinating stories to tell – stories that go back hundreds, if not thousands, of years.

They may be small things, but they have changed our modern world in **BIG** ways.

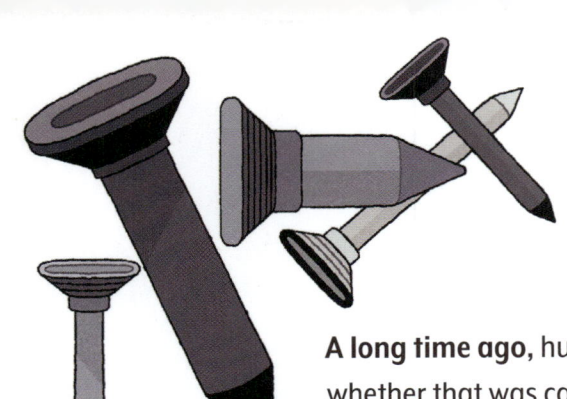

THE NAIL

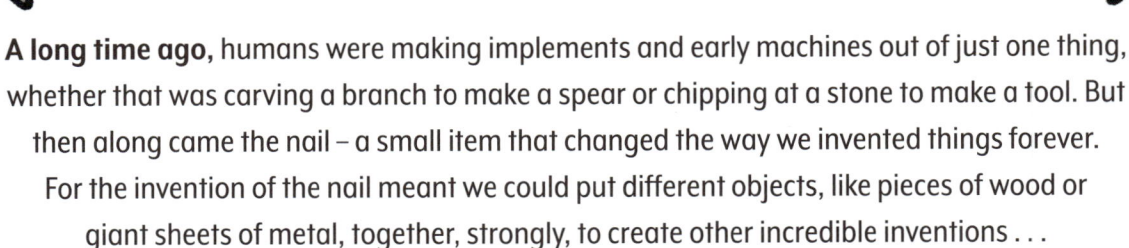

A long time ago, humans were making implements and early machines out of just one thing, whether that was carving a branch to make a spear or chipping at a stone to make a tool. But then along came the nail – a small item that changed the way we invented things forever. For the invention of the nail meant we could put different objects, like pieces of wood or giant sheets of metal, together, strongly, to create other incredible inventions . . .

Around 5,000 years ago and for thousands of years after, the ancient Egyptians hammered a metal called bronze by hand, to create jewelry, decorations and . . . nails. They used the nails to construct boats and chariots.

Around 2,000 years ago, the ancient Roman civilization used a different metal called iron. The iron was made to a high quality in the Indian subcontinent and iron is much stronger than bronze. So, the Romans used iron to make armor, weapons and . . . nails.

Because nails required skilled workers to make them, and used an expensive material, they were really precious. **Around 400 years ago,** nails were so expensive in North America that people used to burn down their wooden houses and collect them, then use them to build their next home.

In 1801, Thomas Jefferson — who went on to become President of the United States — set up a factory, where enslaved men and children made up to 10,000 nails a day. This included Joseph Fossett, who was enslaved as a child and later sent to the nail factory. Joe was only freed after Jefferson died. Jefferson bought a machine that cut iron hoops into nails, speeding up the process of making them.

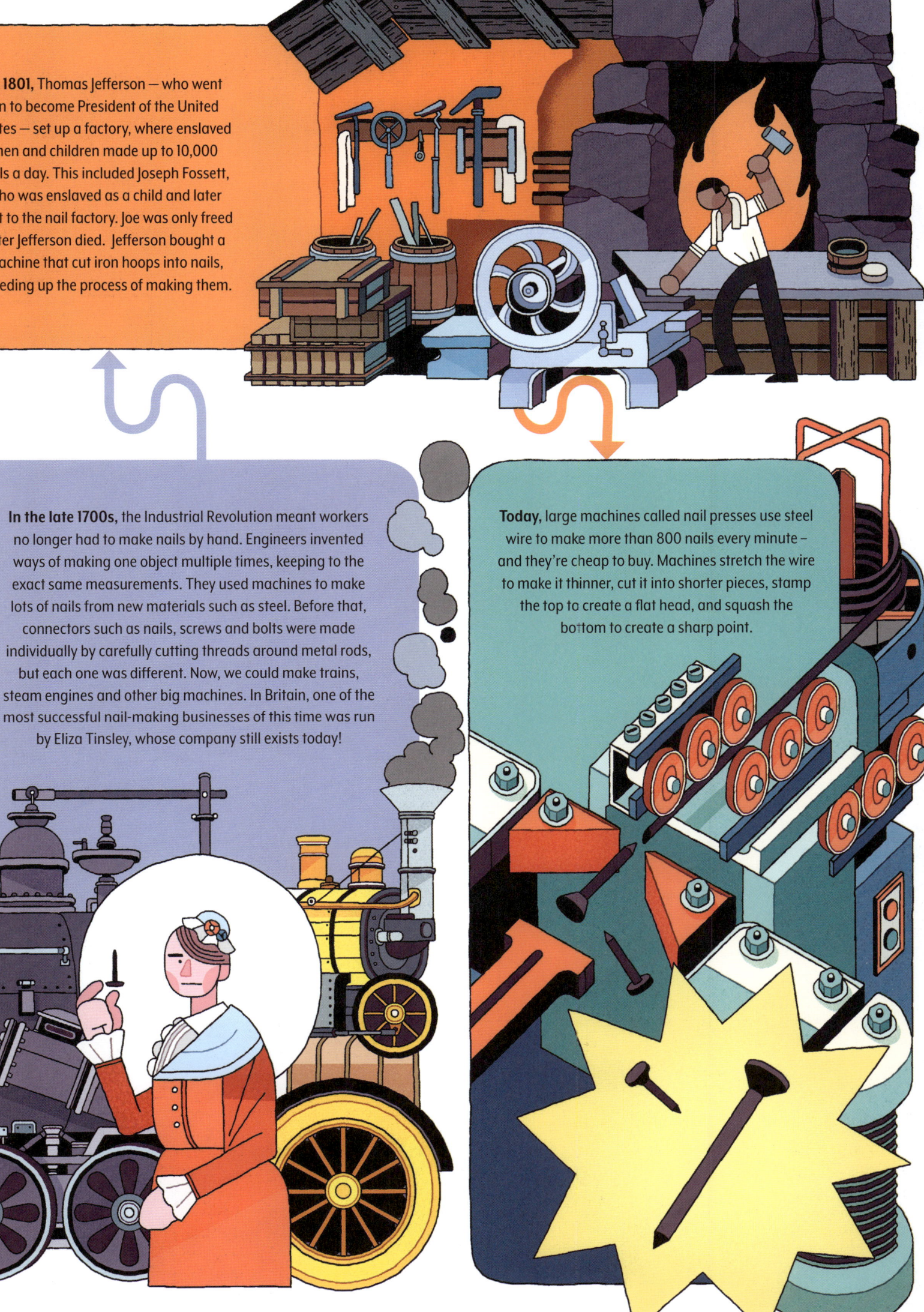

In the late 1700s, the Industrial Revolution meant workers no longer had to make nails by hand. Engineers invented ways of making one object multiple times, keeping to the exact same measurements. They used machines to make lots of nails from new materials such as steel. Before that, connectors such as nails, screws and bolts were made individually by carefully cutting threads around metal rods, but each one was different. Now, we could make trains, steam engines and other big machines. In Britain, one of the most successful nail-making businesses of this time was run by Eliza Tinsley, whose company still exists today!

Today, large machines called nail presses use steel wire to make more than 800 nails every minute – and they're cheap to buy. Machines stretch the wire to make it thinner, cut it into shorter pieces, stamp the top to create a flat head, and squash the bottom to create a sharp point.

7

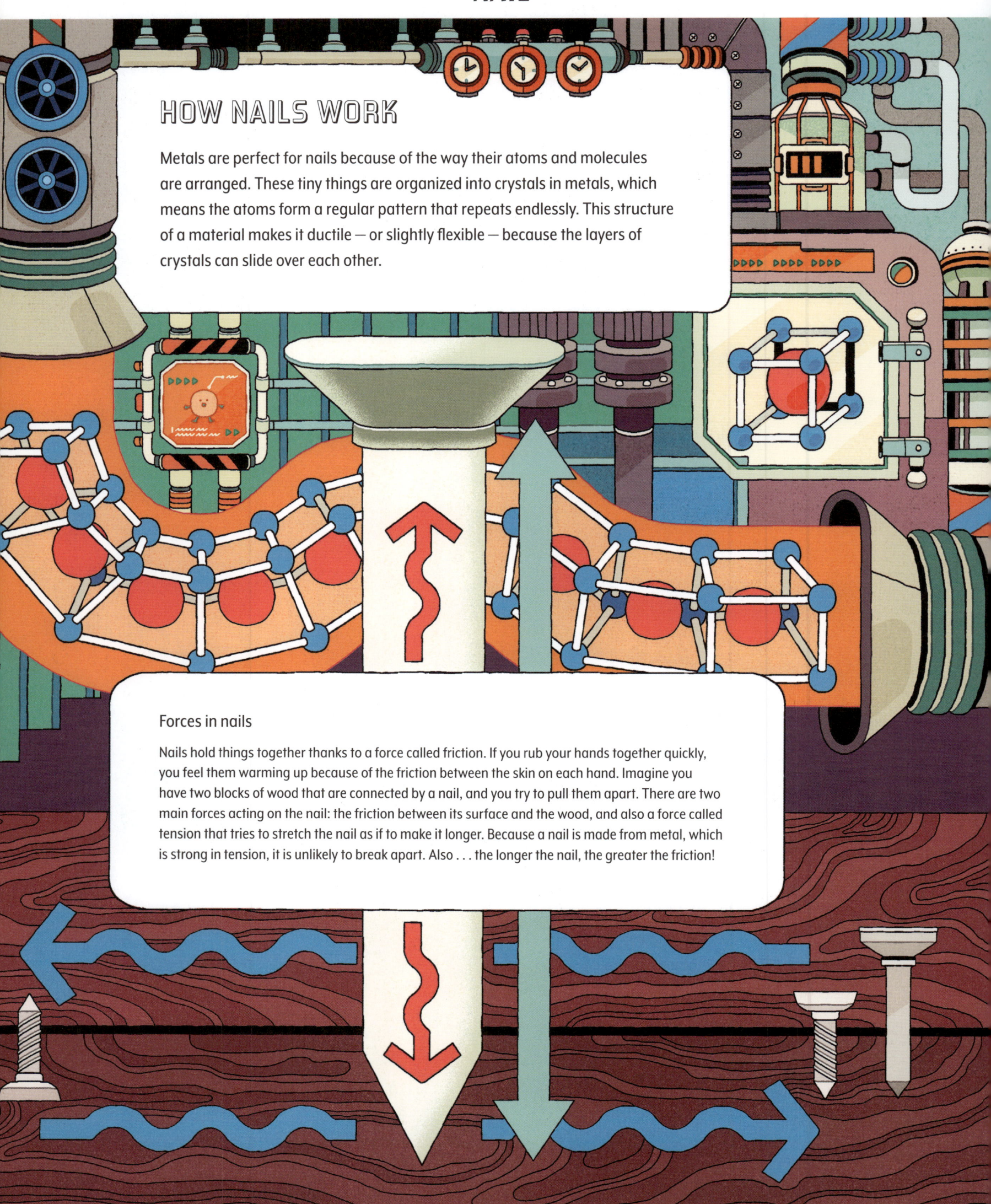

NAIL

HOW NAILS WORK

Metals are perfect for nails because of the way their atoms and molecules are arranged. These tiny things are organized into crystals in metals, which means the atoms form a regular pattern that repeats endlessly. This structure of a material makes it ductile — or slightly flexible — because the layers of crystals can slide over each other.

Forces in nails

Nails hold things together thanks to a force called friction. If you rub your hands together quickly, you feel them warming up because of the friction between the skin on each hand. Imagine you have two blocks of wood that are connected by a nail, and you try to pull them apart. There are two main forces acting on the nail: the friction between its surface and the wood, and also a force called tension that tries to stretch the nail as if to make it longer. Because a nail is made from metal, which is strong in tension, it is unlikely to break apart. Also . . . the longer the nail, the greater the friction!

NAIL

Heating up

When you heat up a metal, the atoms warm up and start bouncing around, slipping and sliding over each other, allowing the heat to move through quickly. This makes the material even more ductile. That's why heating up metals makes them softer, so we can use a hammer to hit the metal and create a sharp point. Different metals behave differently. Copper and bronze become softer at lower temperatures than iron or steel.

Melting down

Combining different metals by melting them and mixing them together creates new materials called alloys. This includes bronze, which is a combination of copper and tin. Steel is also an alloy and is made up of iron, carbon and small quantities of other materials like silicon or phosphorus. Alloys can be stronger than pure metals because when we add in small amounts of *other* metals, the atoms and molecules of the *second* metal lodge themselves within the pure metal's crystals. This means they can't slide as easily over each other, making the material harder.

BUT if you make the metal *too* hard, then it becomes brittle and can crack! The recipe for steel is perfect for creating a strong metal.

Screws, rivets and bolts

The invention of the nail led to the invention of other connectors such as screws, rivets and bolts, which meant we could invent even more cool things – as you're about to discover . . .

SCREW   **BOLT**   **RIVET**

NAIL

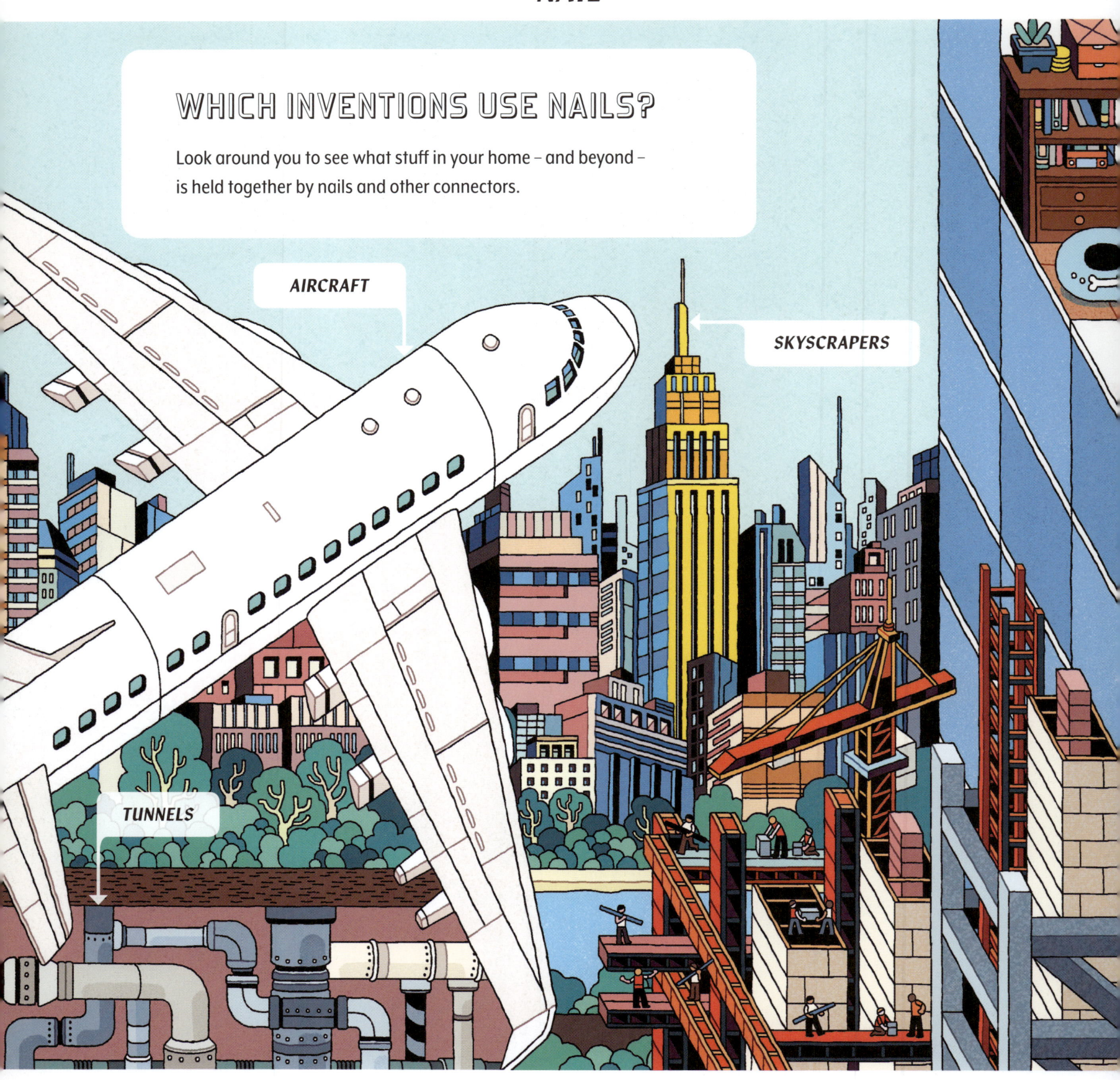

WHICH INVENTIONS USE NAILS?

Look around you to see what stuff in your home – and beyond – is held together by nails and other connectors.

AIRCRAFT

SKYSCRAPERS

TUNNELS

AIRCRAFT
Aircraft use rivets. The rivets are passed through holes in sheets of metal to join them together. Then, the rivet is held in place while one end of the rivet's cylinder is hit and squashed so that the sheets of metal are clamped tight.

SKYSCRAPERS
Bolts are used to construct skyscrapers. Bolts are a combination of screws and rivets. They have a cylindrical shaft with a thread around it, and a hexagonal head.

TUNNELS
Many tunnels are made from rings of iron or steel, which stop soil and water from coming in. These rings are securely joined together with rivets or bolts.

FLOORBOARDS
If you live in an old house with wooden floorboards, you might be able to see the heads of nails, which are similar to the ancient Roman nails.

NAIL

BLENDERS
Blenders, and other household appliances, have lots of screws that hold the different pieces of metal and plastic together securely, even when they shake a lot.

SHOES
Some types of shoes are held together with nails! That might sound dangerous, but they're safely inside the wooden, leather and rubber layers so they won't poke your feet.

LOCKS
Locks can be made with screws. Like nails, screws have a wide head and a narrow body that tapers to a point. Unlike nails, they have a metallic thread that wraps around their bodies.

MICROSCOPES
This invention is held together by many screws. In the base of the microscope there are often four screws, which can be slowly adjusted to make sure the microscope base is perfectly horizontal.

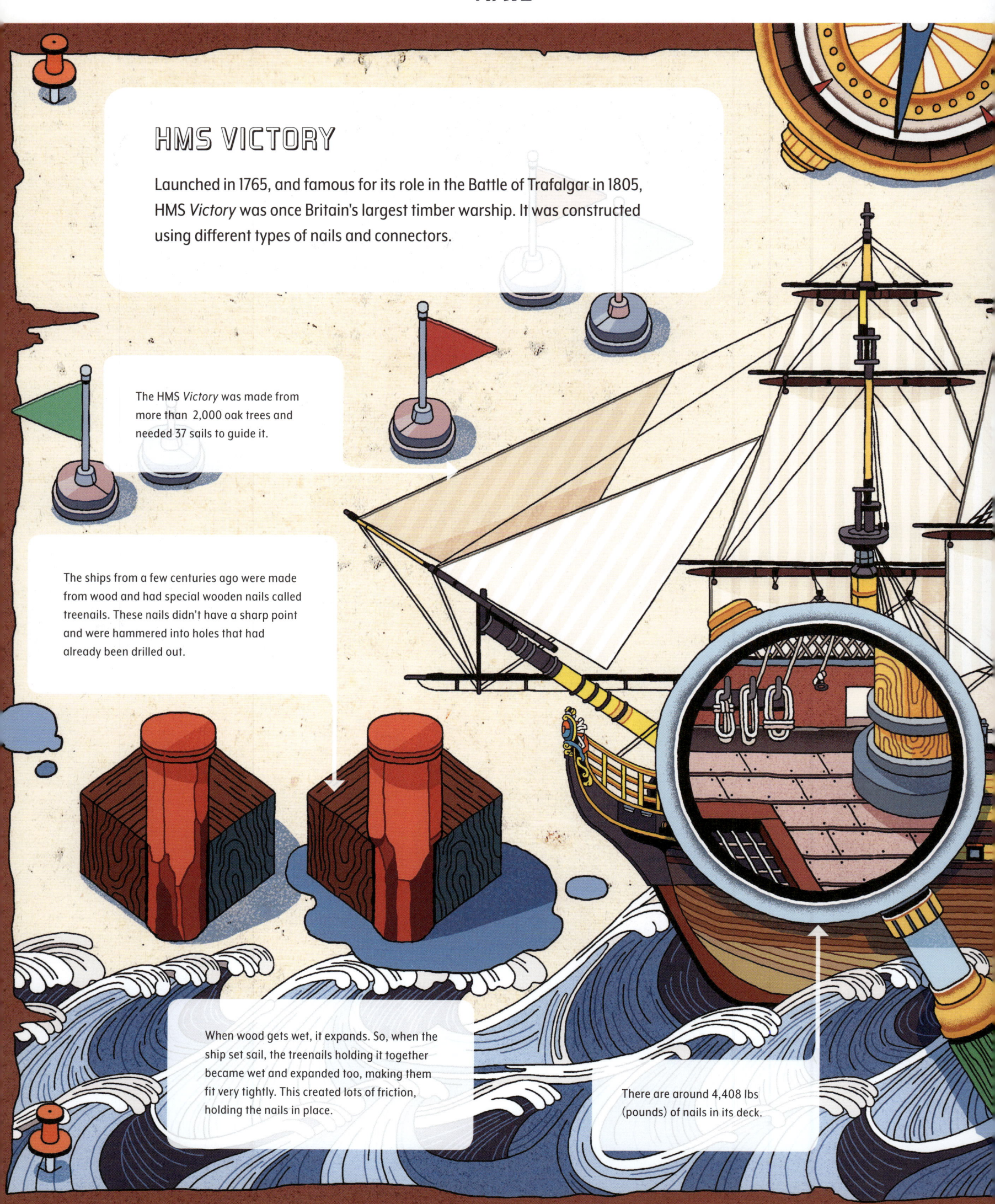

NAIL

HMS VICTORY

Launched in 1765, and famous for its role in the Battle of Trafalgar in 1805, HMS *Victory* was once Britain's largest timber warship. It was constructed using different types of nails and connectors.

The HMS *Victory* was made from more than 2,000 oak trees and needed 37 sails to guide it.

The ships from a few centuries ago were made from wood and had special wooden nails called treenails. These nails didn't have a sharp point and were hammered into holes that had already been drilled out.

When wood gets wet, it expands. So, when the ship set sail, the treenails holding it together became wet and expanded too, making them fit very tightly. This created lots of friction, holding the nails in place.

There are around 4,408 lbs (pounds) of nails in its deck.

NAIL

BRASS NAIL

The Muntz metal spike was a large brass nail with a sharp point.

FORELOCK BOLT

The forelock bolt had a tapered end with a hole in it. A wedge of iron was passed through this hole to lock the bolt in place.

Designed with an L-shaped head, lantern nails were used for hanging lanterns off the wall.

Iron connectors were used above the waterline and inside the ship, where iron would be less prone to rusting.

Engineers used copper connectors under water. Because copper didn't react badly to seawater, it lasted longer.

THE WHEEL

Many human inventions are inspired by nature, such as airplanes (inspired by birds) and Velcro (inspired by seeds with hundreds of tiny hooks). But an entirely human invention (meaning there is nothing like it in nature) is the wheel.

We often think wheels were invented to move us around, but they weren't. **In around 3900 BCE** in ancient Mesopotamia, people wanted to find a way to make bigger and better clay pots, quickly. So they carved a dip into a fixed piece of stone or wood, and, on top of this, they placed a large disk, which had a bulge underneath it. Then, they set the upper disk spinning with their hands. This was the earliest potter's wheel.

Around 2000 BCE, the wheel changed from being a solid disk to having spokes. Now the wheel had a central hub from which a number of cylindrical rods emerged. At the other end of the spokes was the rim of the wheel. These wheels were much lighter but at risk of being shaken apart! This wheel was also used as a symbol in Hindu and Buddhist art and religion.

Then, **sometime around 3500 BCE,** the potter's wheel was turned into an early version of the wheel we see on our cars and trains today. To do that, it required a rod called an axle. The axle passes through a hole in a wheel and allows the wheel to spin around, while the axle holds it in position. We know this happened because archaeologists found tens of thousands of burial mounds in Russia, one of which contained a four-wheeled wagon. It's believed to be one of the earliest wheels in existence.

Then **sometime after 1200 BCE,** a flat metal hoop was added to the outside of the rim while it was hot. This shrunk a little as it cooled and tied the wheel together strongly; this is called the tire.

In the 1800s, aeronautical engineer George Cayley was trying to invent a flying machine. He needed wheels that would allow an aircraft to take off, so he replaced the wooden spokes with many stretched strands of wire to make it lighter. We still see this type of wheel in bicycles today.

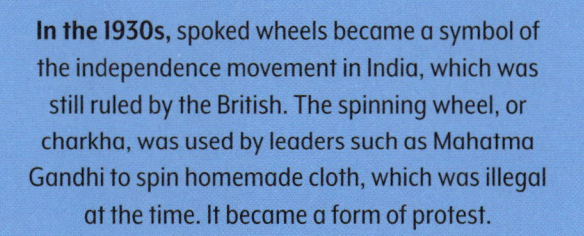

In the 1930s, spoked wheels became a symbol of the independence movement in India, which was still ruled by the British. The spinning wheel, or charkha, was used by leaders such as Mahatma Gandhi to spin homemade cloth, which was illegal at the time. It became a form of protest.

Now that humans can travel by bike, car, truck, train and airplane, we can visit different parts of the world. But the wheel is not just used for travel – it is used in so many other turning, spinning, revolving inventions that you interact with every day . . .

WHEEL

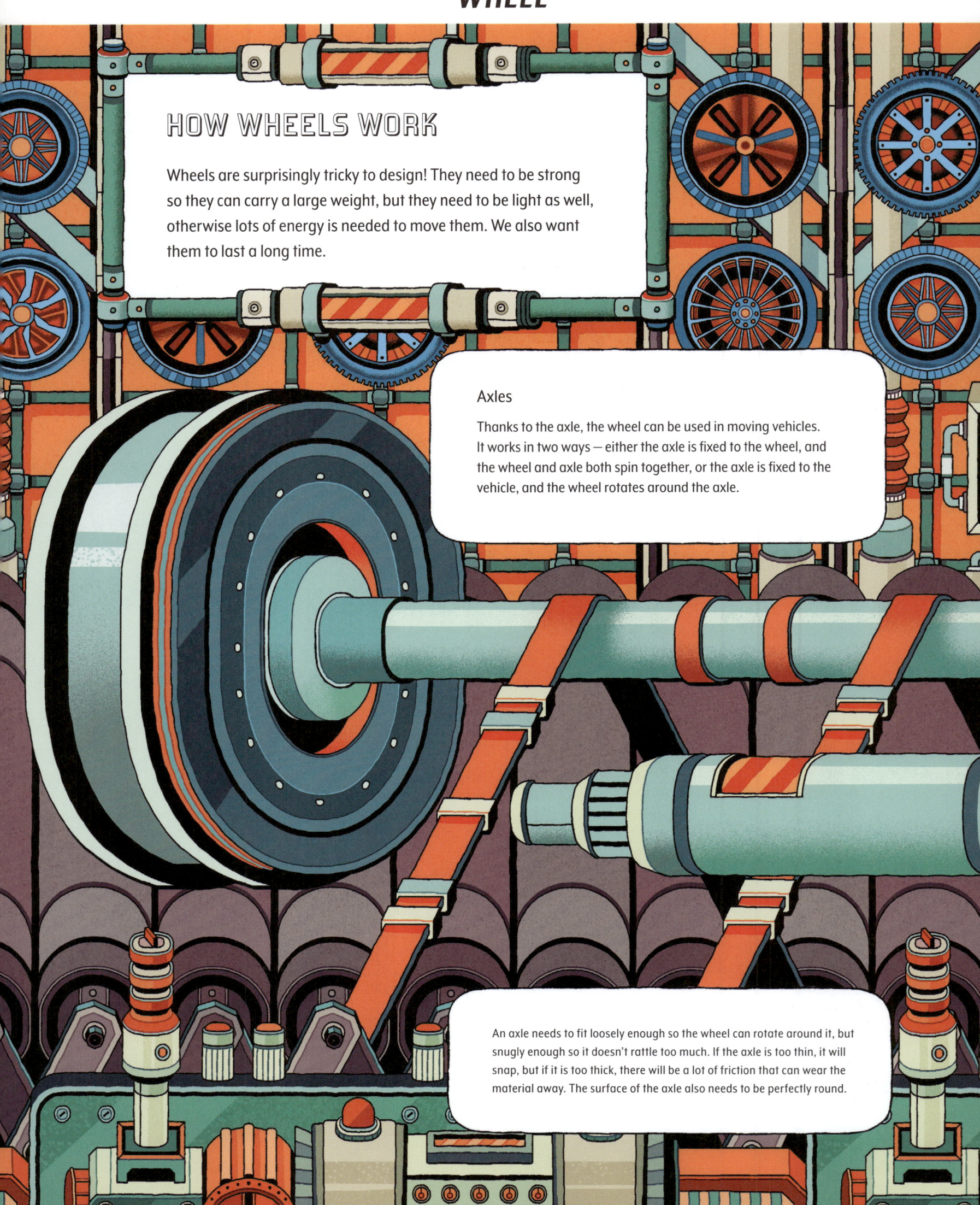

HOW WHEELS WORK

Wheels are surprisingly tricky to design! They need to be strong so they can carry a large weight, but they need to be light as well, otherwise lots of energy is needed to move them. We also want them to last a long time.

Axles

Thanks to the axle, the wheel can be used in moving vehicles. It works in two ways — either the axle is fixed to the wheel, and the wheel and axle both spin together, or the axle is fixed to the vehicle, and the wheel rotates around the axle.

An axle needs to fit loosely enough so the wheel can rotate around it, but snugly enough so it doesn't rattle too much. If the axle is too thin, it will snap, but if it is too thick, there will be a lot of friction that can wear the material away. The surface of the axle also needs to be perfectly round.

WHEEL

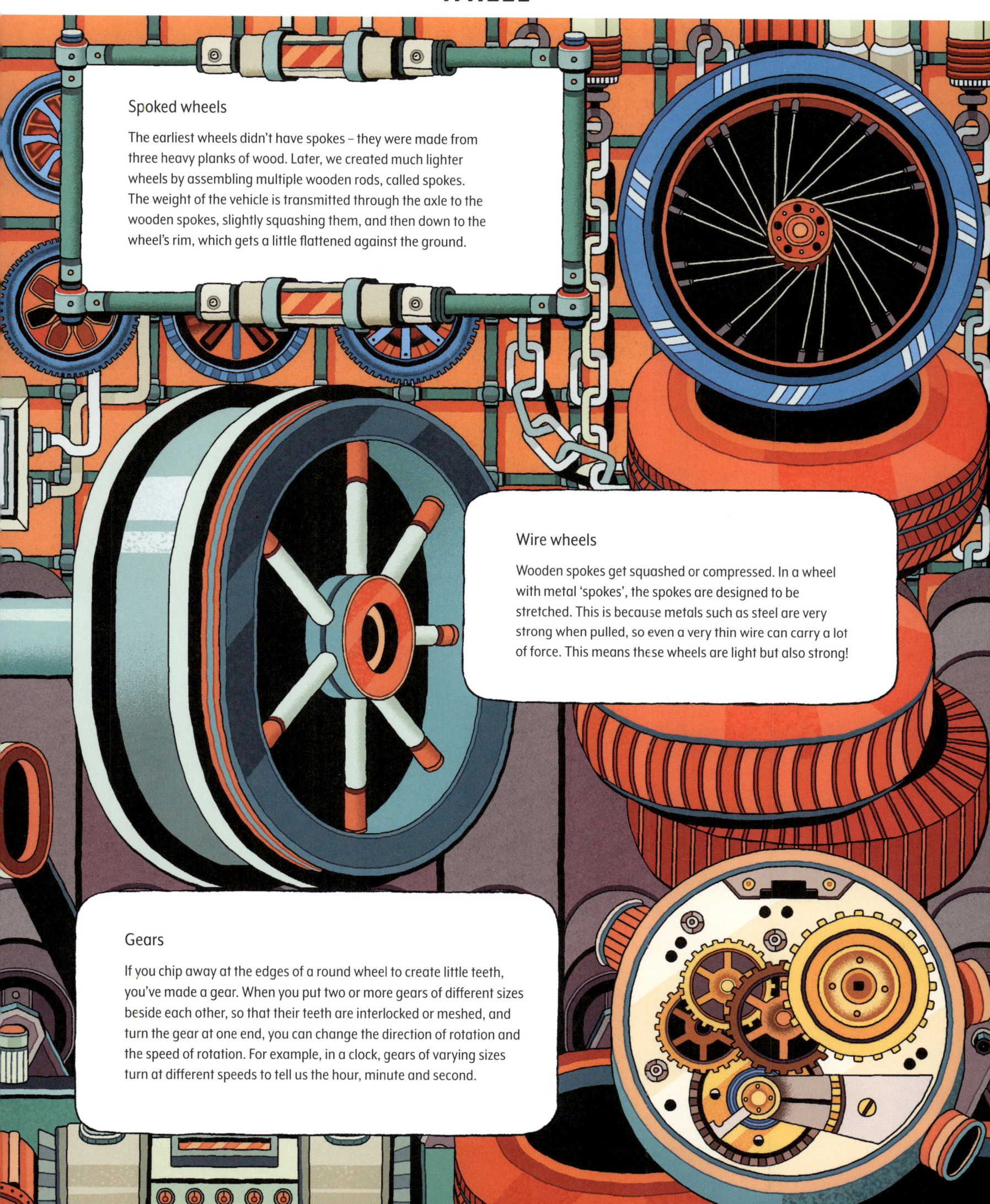

Spoked wheels

The earliest wheels didn't have spokes – they were made from three heavy planks of wood. Later, we created much lighter wheels by assembling multiple wooden rods, called spokes. The weight of the vehicle is transmitted through the axle to the wooden spokes, slightly squashing them, and then down to the wheel's rim, which gets a little flattened against the ground.

Wire wheels

Wooden spokes get squashed or compressed. In a wheel with metal 'spokes', the spokes are designed to be stretched. This is because metals such as steel are very strong when pulled, so even a very thin wire can carry a lot of force. This means these wheels are light but also strong!

Gears

If you chip away at the edges of a round wheel to create little teeth, you've made a gear. When you put two or more gears of different sizes beside each other, so that their teeth are interlocked or meshed, and turn the gear at one end, you can change the direction of rotation and the speed of rotation. For example, in a clock, gears of varying sizes turn at different speeds to tell us the hour, minute and second.

WHEEL

WHICH INVENTIONS USE WHEELS?

Plenty of amazing inventions from the distant past right up to the modern day only work because of wheels . . .

ASTROLABES

A scientist called Mariam al-Asturlabi designed and made some amazing astrolabes!

PEN POINTS

FIDGET SPINNERS

SKATEBOARDS

SKATEBOARDS
Skateboards have small and slighty squishy wheels at their base. This little bit of flexibility lets you jump around at different angles without breaking the wheels.

FIDGET SPINNERS
At the center of a fidget spinner are two rings with balls between them. When you set the spinner off, these balls act like wheels, rolling around and rotating the main body of the spinner.

ASTROLABES
The astrolabe is a metal or wooden disk with a bar at its center called the alidade. By lining the bar up with the Sun*, Moon or a star and measuring the number of degrees around the circle, astronomers were able to measure the position of the objects in the night sky.

*You should never look directly at the Sun.

PEN POINTS
A ballpoint pen features a tiny sphere at the bottom of the long, thin ink cartridge. The sphere rolls around and pulls ink down onto the paper. The sphere is like a 3D wheel!

WHEEL

DISHWASHERS

TRAINS

ELECTRIC TOOTHBRUSHES

DOORKNOBS

DISHWASHERS
Josephine Cochran invented the first automatic dishwasher. It works thanks to an arrangement of spinning baskets and moving gears, which most modern machines are still based on.

ELECTRIC TOOTHBRUSHES
The head of an electric toothbrush uses a spinning action (similar to a wheel) to wipe away all that plaque on your teeth!

DOORKNOBS
Doorknobs are often shaped into spheres, which is a nice shape to hold in our hands. Spheres are like three-dimensional wheels that can turn and create movement.

TRAINS
Trains have lots of small wheels that keep them running on their tracks. They also have gears that transfer power into the wheels to make them move forward.

WHEEL

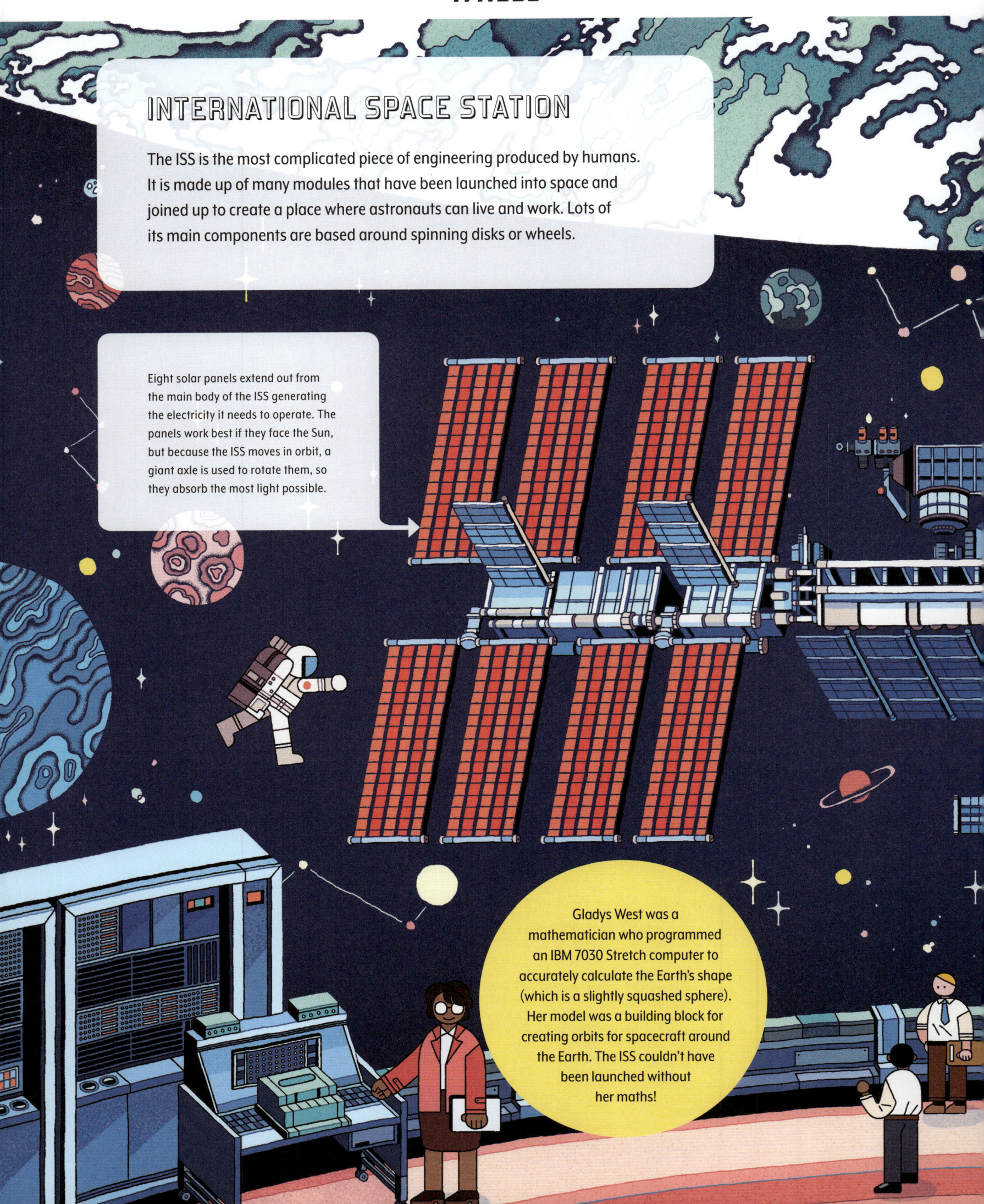

INTERNATIONAL SPACE STATION

The ISS is the most complicated piece of engineering produced by humans. It is made up of many modules that have been launched into space and joined up to create a place where astronauts can live and work. Lots of its main components are based around spinning disks or wheels.

Eight solar panels extend out from the main body of the ISS generating the electricity it needs to operate. The panels work best if they face the Sun, but because the ISS moves in orbit, a giant axle is used to rotate them, so they absorb the most light possible.

Gladys West was a mathematician who programmed an IBM 7030 Stretch computer to accurately calculate the Earth's shape (which is a slightly squashed sphere). Her model was a building block for creating orbits for spacecraft around the Earth. The ISS couldn't have been launched without her maths!

WHEEL

The ISS follows a carefully calculated orbit around the Earth. To keep it perfectly aligned (or to make sure it doesn't go off orbit) it is controlled by a group of four special wheels called Control Moment Gyroscopes (CMG).

The CMG wheels are a bit like spinning tops. If you set a top spinning, it balances itself on a small tip thanks to something called momentum. If it isn't spinning, it falls over because there is no momentum.

THE SPRING

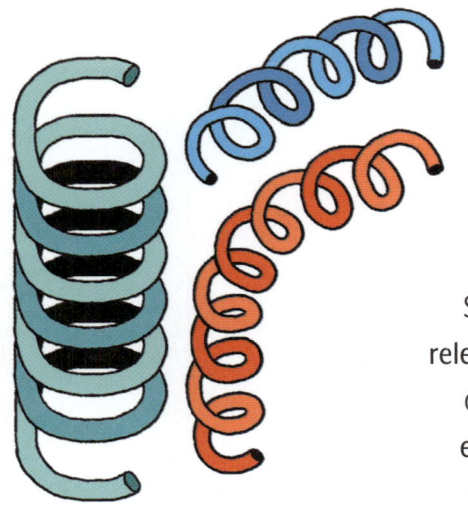

Springs are wonderful inventions that humans created to store and release energy. When a force is applied, a spring is pulled back or pushed down and energy is created. When the spring is released again, the energy is released too, creating movement. Springs come in a range of different shapes and sizes, and they are not always coil-shaped.

We think one of the earliest examples of a spring is the Holmegaard bow, which was found in Denmark by archaeologists. It is **10,000 years old,** but humans have been using this weapon far longer. An impressive example of an engineered bow is the one used by Genghis Khan, the Emperor of Mongolia from 1206 till 1227 CE. Mongolian archers made extremely flexible bows using bamboo at the center, with fibres from the tendons of animals' legs stuck on one side, and boiled bone on the other.

Around 3000 BCE, people in Mesopotamia, India and Egypt created tweezers by bending a ribbon of copper or bronze into a narrow U-shape. Tweezers are a type of spring; they are made using a flexible material that changes shape when you put force on it (squeeze them together). These ancient tweezers might have been used to remove splinters, thorns or arrows from your body, or to catch lice! These inspired some of the tools that are used in surgery today.

Around 2000 years ago, the Romans also used tweezers, but for a different purpose. A letter from the famous ancient Roman author, Seneca, to his friend complains about the screams of men from public baths who were having their armpits plucked.

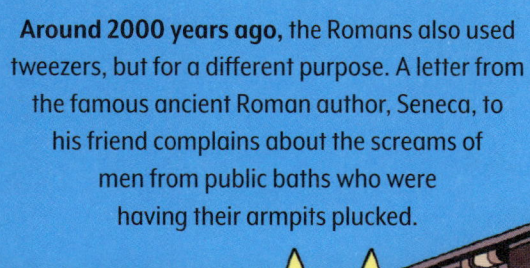

Then in the **late 1600s**, Robert Hooke explained how to calculate the strength of springs and how much they would change shape depending on the weight put on them. This led to the springs we know today — coiled metal ones.

$F=kx$

In the last 400 years, springs were also used by coach-makers. Their leaf springs were banana-shaped and created from layers of metal that made rides in horse-drawn carriages less bumpy.

And **about 100 years later,** springs were being used in many ways. Springs meant clocks were small and accurate for the first time. They created locks for our homes that were really difficult to pick. These sorts of springs needed to be carefully made to the perfect size, which became possible thanks to the factories that *sprang* up during the Industrial Revolution.

SPRING

HOW SPRINGS WORK

Springs are made from a flexible material that can be deformed, meaning a spring's shape can be changed. When deformed, it stores energy, which is released when it goes back to its original shape. We can use that energy to do useful things. For example, if we pull on the string of a bow to curve it more, then release it, the energy is transferred into the arrow, which shoots off into the distance.

Extensions and forces

Robert Hooke was born in 1635 in England and was interested in machines. He wanted to explain mathematically how springs work, so he published his theory as a puzzle in 1660 and only explained it properly 18 years later! The latin puzzle said *'ut tensio, sic vis'*, which means, 'as the extension, so the force'.

What he meant was this: if you have a spring that extends by 1 centimetre (cm) when a weight of 1 kg is added to it, then a weight of 2 kg will cause a 2 cm extension. This law works as long as the spring is not stretched so far that it permanently deforms or breaks.

For coiled metal springs, for example, we use Hooke's mathematical equation to calculate how tall and wide springs need to be, how many coils they need, how thick the wire should be, and how much they will deform under the forces they will feel.

$$F = kx$$

SPRING

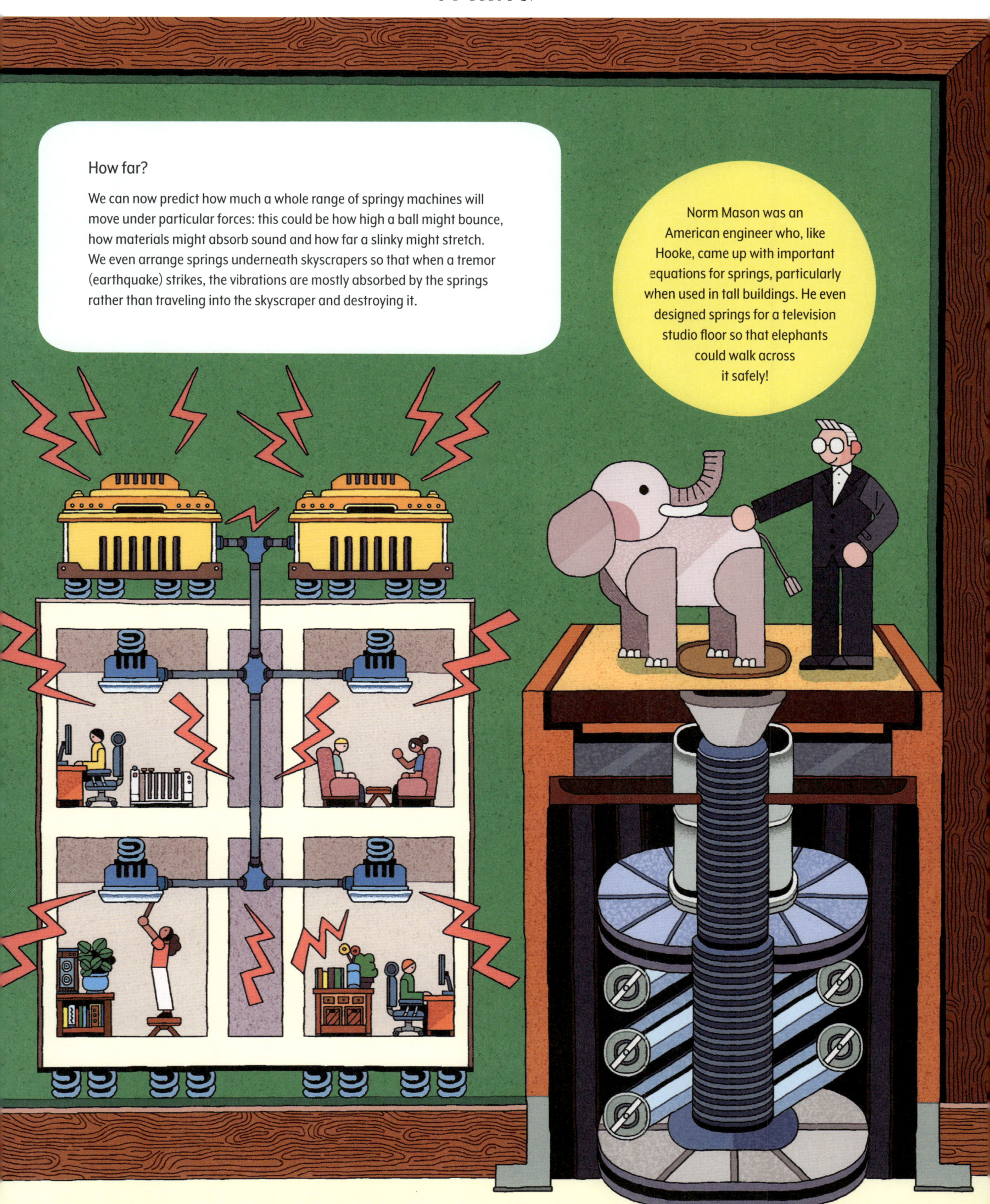

How far?

We can now predict how much a whole range of springy machines will move under particular forces: this could be how high a ball might bounce, how materials might absorb sound and how far a slinky might stretch. We even arrange springs underneath skyscrapers so that when a tremor (earthquake) strikes, the vibrations are mostly absorbed by the springs rather than traveling into the skyscraper and destroying it.

Norm Mason was an American engineer who, like Hooke, came up with important equations for springs, particularly when used in tall buildings. He even designed springs for a television studio floor so that elephants could walk across it safely!

SPRING

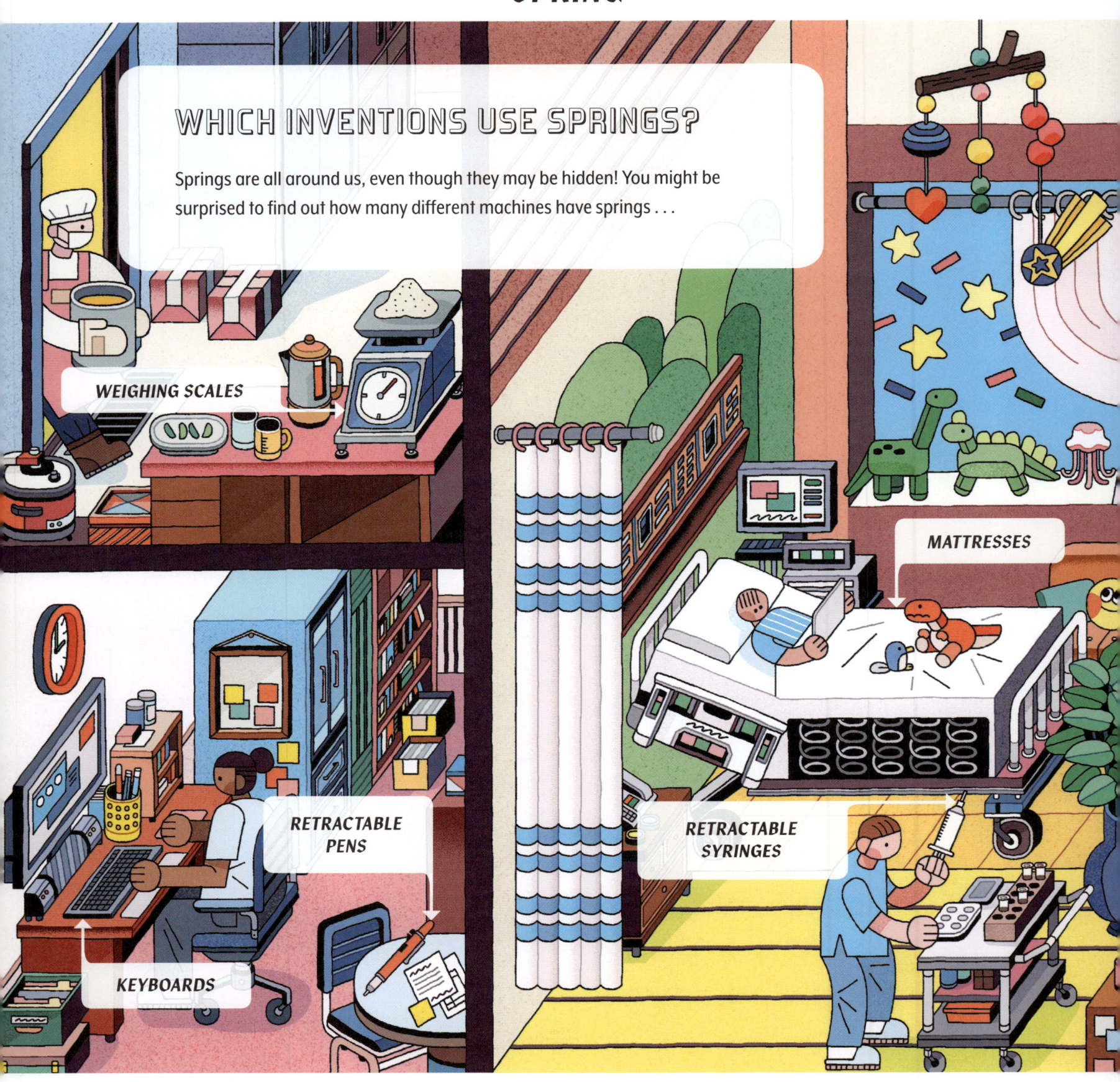

WHICH INVENTIONS USE SPRINGS?

Springs are all around us, even though they may be hidden! You might be surprised to find out how many different machines have springs . . .

WEIGHING SCALES

MATTRESSES

RETRACTABLE PENS

KEYBOARDS

RETRACTABLE SYRINGES

WEIGHING SCALES
When baking, you might need to measure how much flour you need. The weight of the flour pushes down on the scale and compresses a spring, which turns a needle to tell you the answer.

KEYBOARDS
Every key on a keyboard – in fact any type of push button – has a small spring below it.

RETRACTABLE PENS
Pushing down on the button at the top of a retractable (clicky) pen makes the ink cartridge squash the spring at the bottom, which forces the nib of the pen to poke out. A small lever locks it in place so you can write.

RETRACTABLE SYRINGES
Safety syringes are a type of injector where the needle gets pulled back inside the syringe by a spring after it's been used.

SPRING

BASES FOR MICROSCOPES AND TELESCOPEES

SLINKYS

TRAMPOLINES

MATTRESSES
Many mattresses have lots of big springs hidden inside to support our bodies and help us sleep well.

SLINKYS
Slinkys are springs that have lots and lots of coils very close together, and are quite flexible. Because of their size and stiffness, they can 'walk' down the stairs!

TRAMPOLINES
There are strong springs all around trampolines that stretch when we jump on them. The energy from the springs releases back into the trampoline and into us, sending us high up.

BASES FOR MICROSCOPES AND TELESCOPES
If microscopes or telescopes shake, you can't see what you're looking at properly. Small sensitive springs in their bases absorb vibrations to make sure you have a clear view.

27

SPRING

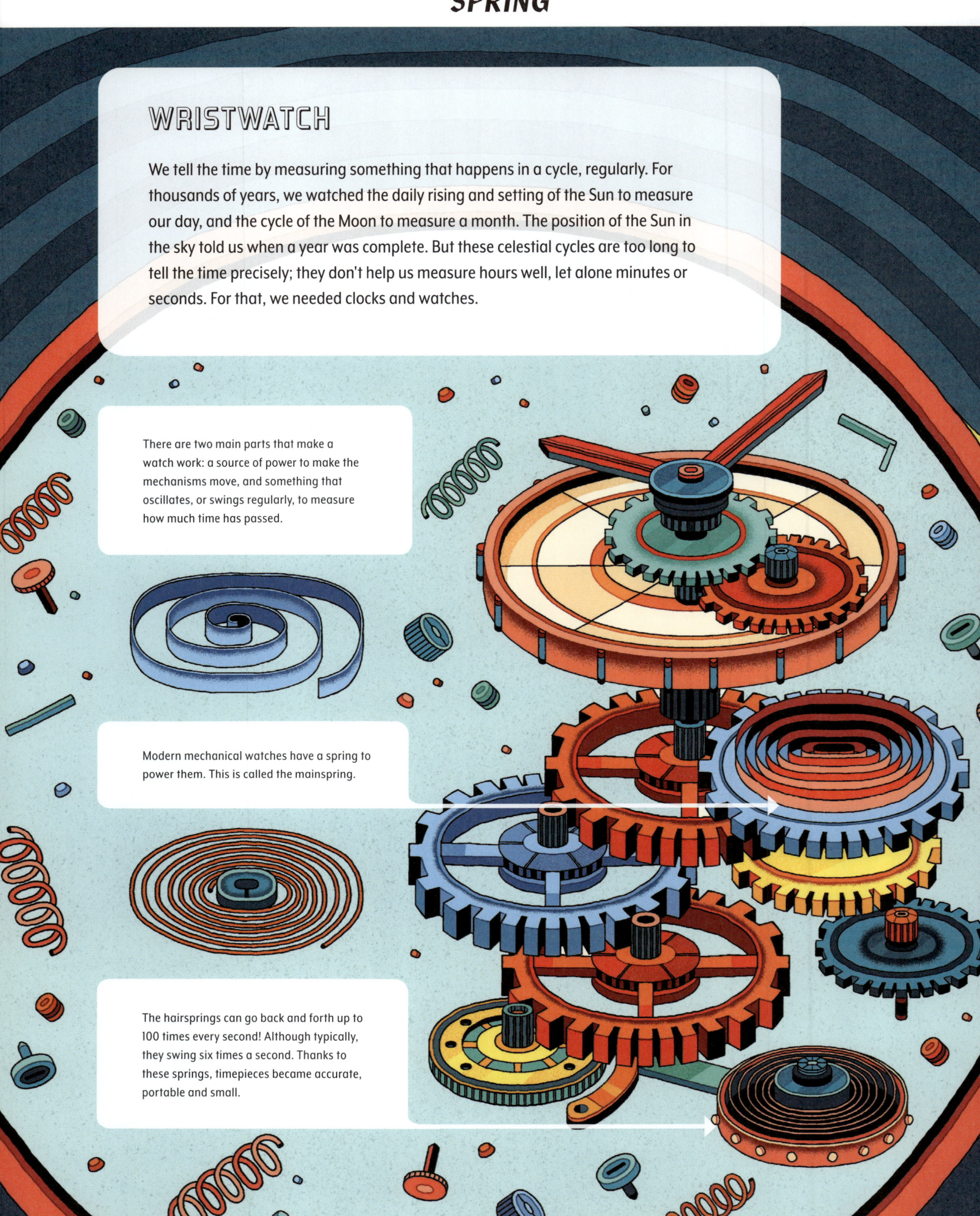

WRISTWATCH

We tell the time by measuring something that happens in a cycle, regularly. For thousands of years, we watched the daily rising and setting of the Sun to measure our day, and the cycle of the Moon to measure a month. The position of the Sun in the sky told us when a year was complete. But these celestial cycles are too long to tell the time precisely; they don't help us measure hours well, let alone minutes or seconds. For that, we needed clocks and watches.

There are two main parts that make a watch work: a source of power to make the mechanisms move, and something that oscillates, or swings regularly, to measure how much time has passed.

Modern mechanical watches have a spring to power them. This is called the mainspring.

The hairsprings can go back and forth up to 100 times every second! Although typically, they swing six times a second. Thanks to these springs, timepieces became accurate, portable and small.

SPRING

Rebecca Struthers is a watchmaker, and the first in UK history to get a PhD in horology, the study of time, clocks and watches. She and her partner Craig run a business called Struthers Watchmakers where they use old machines to make beautiful watches and restore historic timepieces.

This invention is important because scientists need to measure time accurately to track the movement of the Sun, Moon and other celestial bodies (things in space).

Trains need to know the exact time so they don't end up on the same tracks as each other.

The invention of watches allowed ships to travel safely and map the world!

29

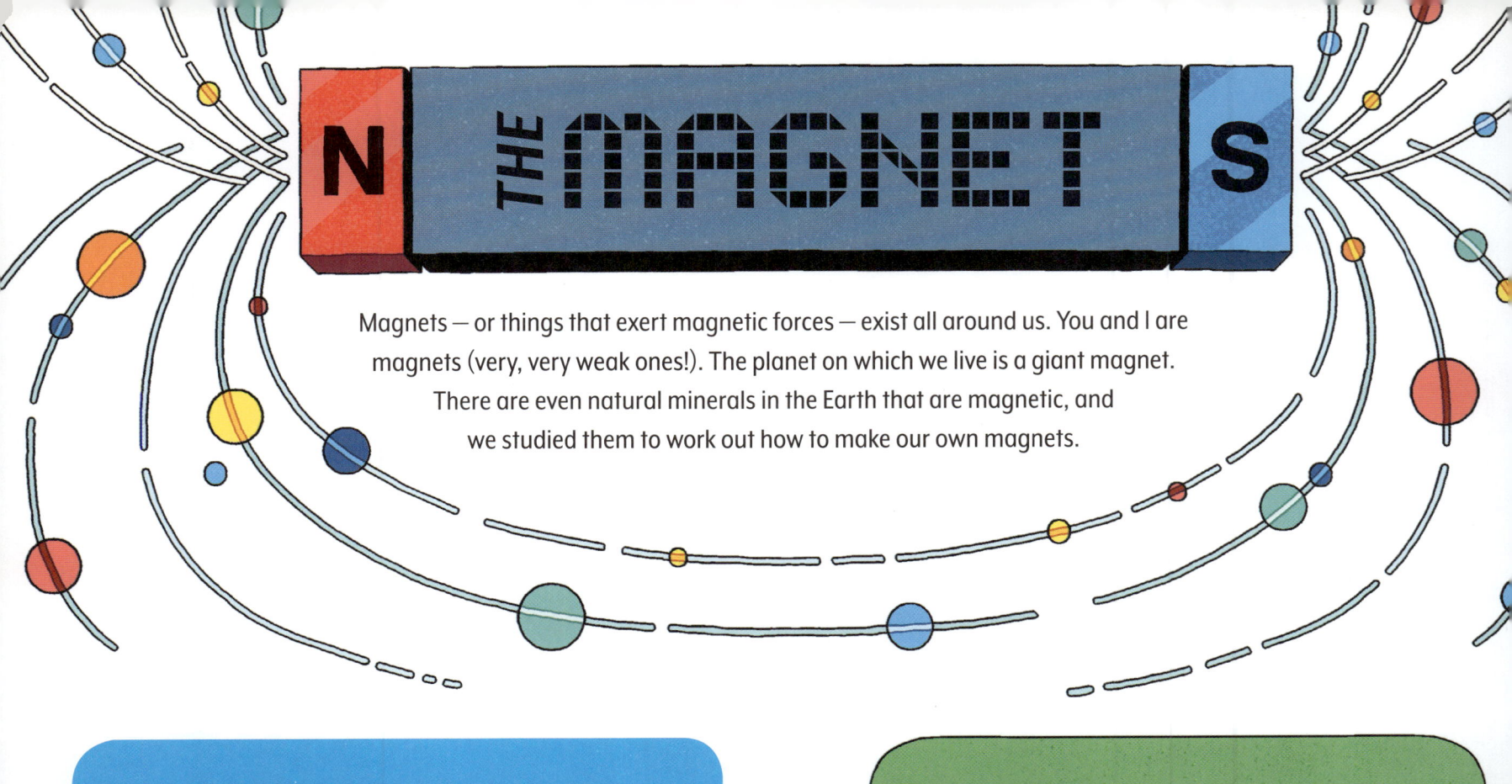

THE MAGNET

Magnets — or things that exert magnetic forces — exist all around us. You and I are magnets (very, very weak ones!). The planet on which we live is a giant magnet. There are even natural minerals in the Earth that are magnetic, and we studied them to work out how to make our own magnets.

Thousands of years ago, humans discovered a material known as lodestone that was magnetic. Lodestone is a type of magnetite, a natural mineral found in the earth, with a mix of iron, oxygen and other impurities. It is rare and its natural magnetism is weak.

Around 2,600 years ago, the ancient Greeks wrote about this material in their texts. Two hundred years later, the Chinese noted that lodestone attracts iron.

Over a thousand years later, lodestone was used for navigation in the form of a compass. Navigators in the Song dynasty in China shaped lodestone to look like a fish, and let it float freely in water so it pointed south. This knowledge spread to Europe and the Middle East.

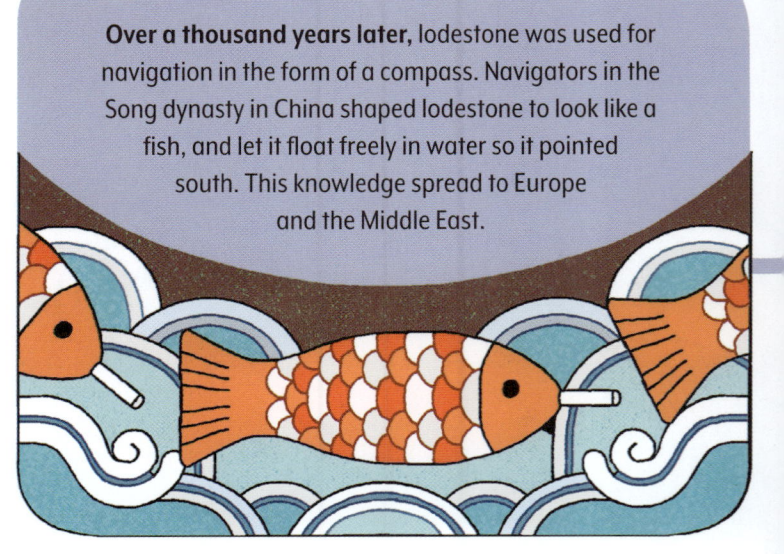

In 1926, Japanese engineer Kenjiro Takayanagi invented the first electric television with the help of magnets. He used a cathode ray tube, a machine that sends out a stream of electrons that are moved around using a magnetic field. The moving electron beam hit a glass screen and lit it up to create moving images.

Finally, **in the nineteenth century,** we discovered electromagnetism, which allows us to move electrons (parts of atoms) to create and change magnetic force and apply it to our technology. This discovery also helped us discover the secrets of our universe.

And **in the 1940s,** ceramic magnets were created by pressing together tiny balls of barium or strontium with iron. These are the ones we use most today; rare-earth magnets are made from elements such as samarium, cerium, yttrium, praseodymium and others.

It was only in the **last hundred years** or so that we could study and manipulate atoms (the building blocks of matter) to make strong, long-lasting magnets.

Now we are discovering new ways to make permanent magnets by heating up and then squashing different materials together. We do this to make magnets that are used in cars.

31

MAGNET

HOW MAGNETS WORK

To grasp the science of magnetism, first we must understand how atoms work. That is why it took thousands of years of study before we worked out the materials and forces behind magnets. Atoms are the tiny building blocks of matter – they make up everything in our universe. An atom is made up of a nucleus in the center, and electrons orbiting around it – a bit like how the Moon orbits Earth.

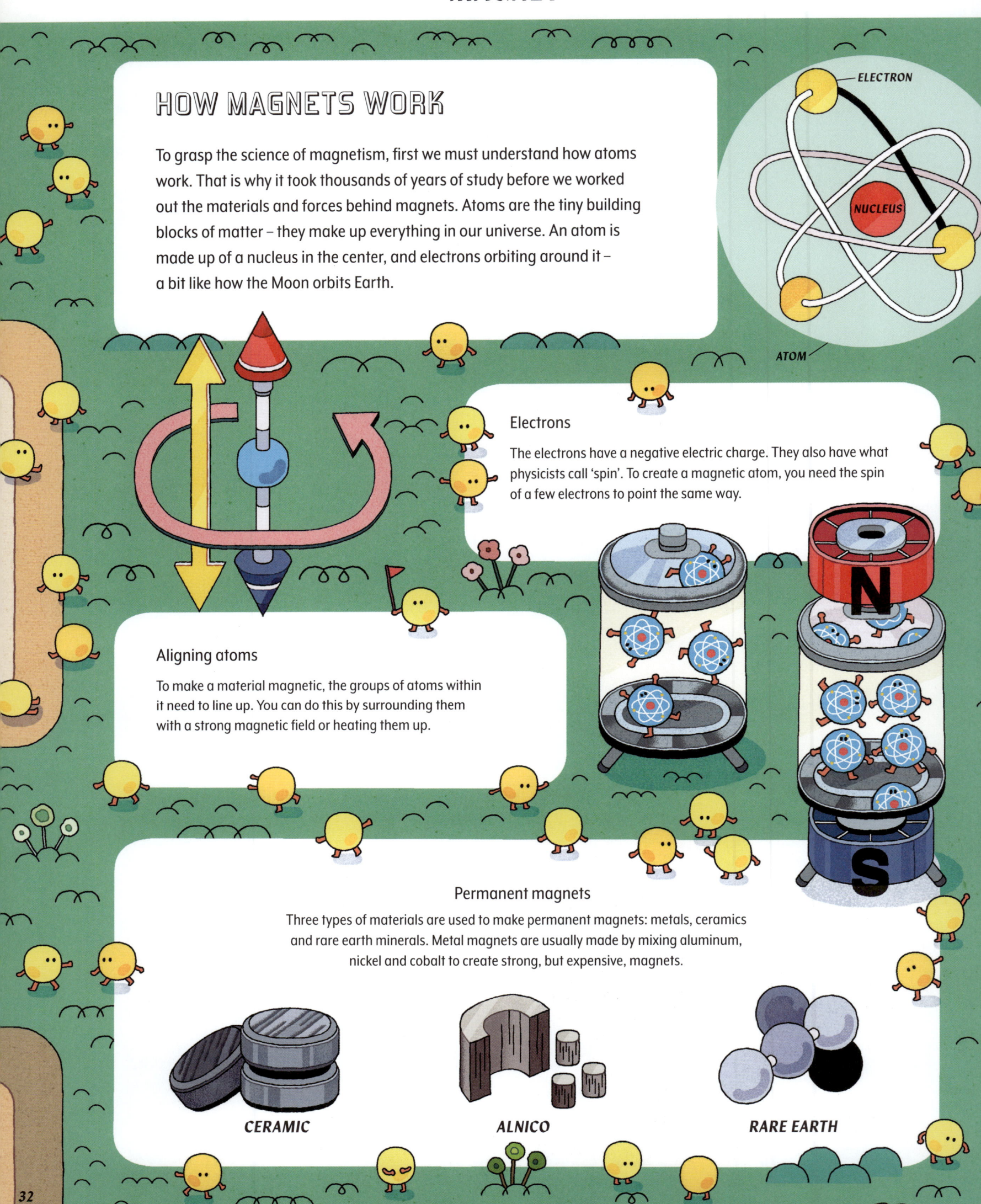

ELECTRON
NUCLEUS
ATOM

Electrons

The electrons have a negative electric charge. They also have what physicists call 'spin'. To create a magnetic atom, you need the spin of a few electrons to point the same way.

Aligning atoms

To make a material magnetic, the groups of atoms within it need to line up. You can do this by surrounding them with a strong magnetic field or heating them up.

Permanent magnets

Three types of materials are used to make permanent magnets: metals, ceramics and rare earth minerals. Metal magnets are usually made by mixing aluminum, nickel and cobalt to create strong, but expensive, magnets.

CERAMIC **ALNICO** **RARE EARTH**

MAGNET

Electromagnets

Like gravity, electromagnetism is one of the four fundamental forces in nature (the other two are the 'weak force' and the 'strong force'). To create an electromagnet, you surround a piece of iron or steel with a coil of thin metal wire, and when you pass electricity through the coil, the metal becomes magnetic. If you switch off the current, the magnetism disappears. So, electromagnets are perfect where we need to control how strong a magnet is, or for when we need to switch a magnet on and off. A hairdryer uses an electromagnet in its motor.

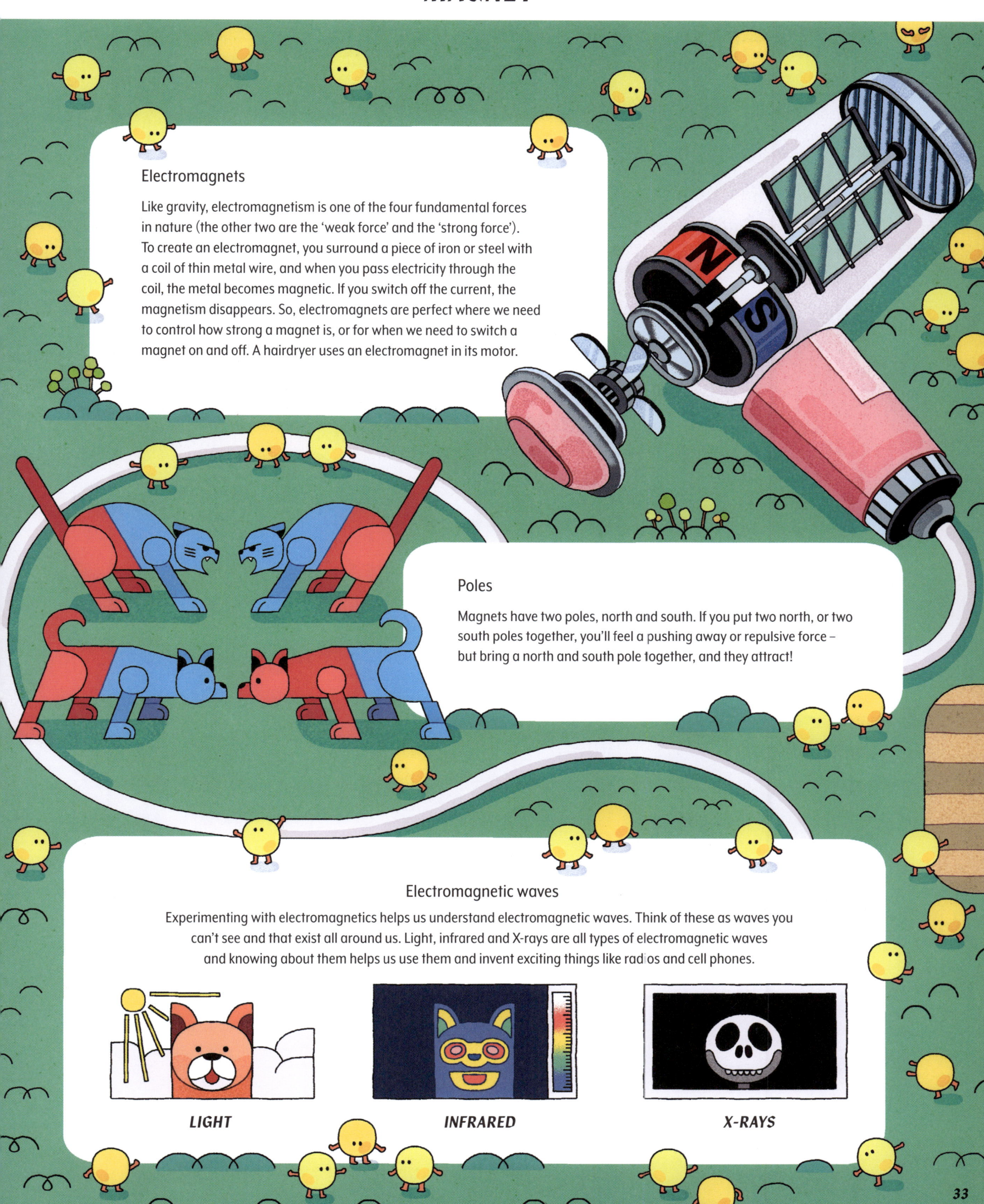

Poles

Magnets have two poles, north and south. If you put two north, or two south poles together, you'll feel a pushing away or repulsive force – but bring a north and south pole together, and they attract!

Electromagnetic waves

Experimenting with electromagnetics helps us understand electromagnetic waves. Think of these as waves you can't see and that exist all around us. Light, infrared and X-rays are all types of electromagnetic waves and knowing about them helps us use them and invent exciting things like radios and cell phones.

LIGHT **INFRARED** **X-RAYS**

MAGNET

WHICH INVENTIONS USE MAGNETS?

All these things have been invented thanks to our understanding of magnets . . .

RADIOS

SPEAKERS

PRINTERS

PRINTERS
The printers that print receipts in a shop or tickets in a station have small pins on the end of tiny hammers held by springs. A permanent magnet keeps the hammer in place. An electric current creates a field that pushes the hammer towards the paper, and the pin makes a small dot.

RADIOS
Radios receive sound from radio stations thanks to electromagnetic waves. In 1895, Indian scientist Jagadish Chandra Bose showed that such waves could travel over very long distances and transfer messages.

SPEAKERS
Speakers receive an electrical current that varies, and this current generates a magnetic field. This field then makes a cylinder and a sheet called the 'coil' and 'diaphragm' vibrate – vibrations produce sound.

TELEPHONES
The original telephones used a rapidly changing electrical current to form a rapidly changing magnetic field. This created vibrations in an iron disk, which turned into sound.

MAGNET

MAGLEV TRAINS

THERMOSTATS

WIRELESS CHARGERS

HARD DRIVES

TELEPHONES

MAGLEV TRAINS
This train floats just above its tracks. If you put the north poles of two magnets close to each other, the magnets push away. The same idea is used in maglev – or magnetic levitation – trains, where powerful electromagnets create this pushing force between the train and the tracks, making it move – fast.

WIRELESS CHARGERS
We can transmit electricity through the air by creating a magnetic field between two electrical circuits. This technology is now used to charge phones, laptops and our electrical toothbrushes.

HARD DRIVES
Hard drives are coated in a magnetic material called iron oxide. Since magnets have two poles – north and south – an electromagnet is used to force tiny zones of this coating to point in different directions, stor ng data. Another electromagnet 'reads' the directions of the millions of little zones and feeds it back to the computer as binary code (also known as '0s and 1s'), a language that computers know how to read.

THERMOSTATS
A thermostat sets the temperature of the heating or air conditioning in our homes. Electronic thermostats have a switch called a magnetic relay. In the off position, the relay breaks the circuit, so no power goes into the heating/cooling system. To switch it on, an electrical pulse is sent to the relay, which activates the magnet to close the circuit.

MAGNET

THE LARGE HADRON COLLIDER

The Large Hadron Collider (LHC) at CERN, the European Council for Nuclear Research, is the world's largest particle accelerator – it moves particles around *super* fast and then makes them collide to see what will happen.

Scientists use the LHC to investigate matter and the origins of the universe by studying tiny particles that make up atoms. They do this by creating explosive collisions between beams of these particles.

MAGNET

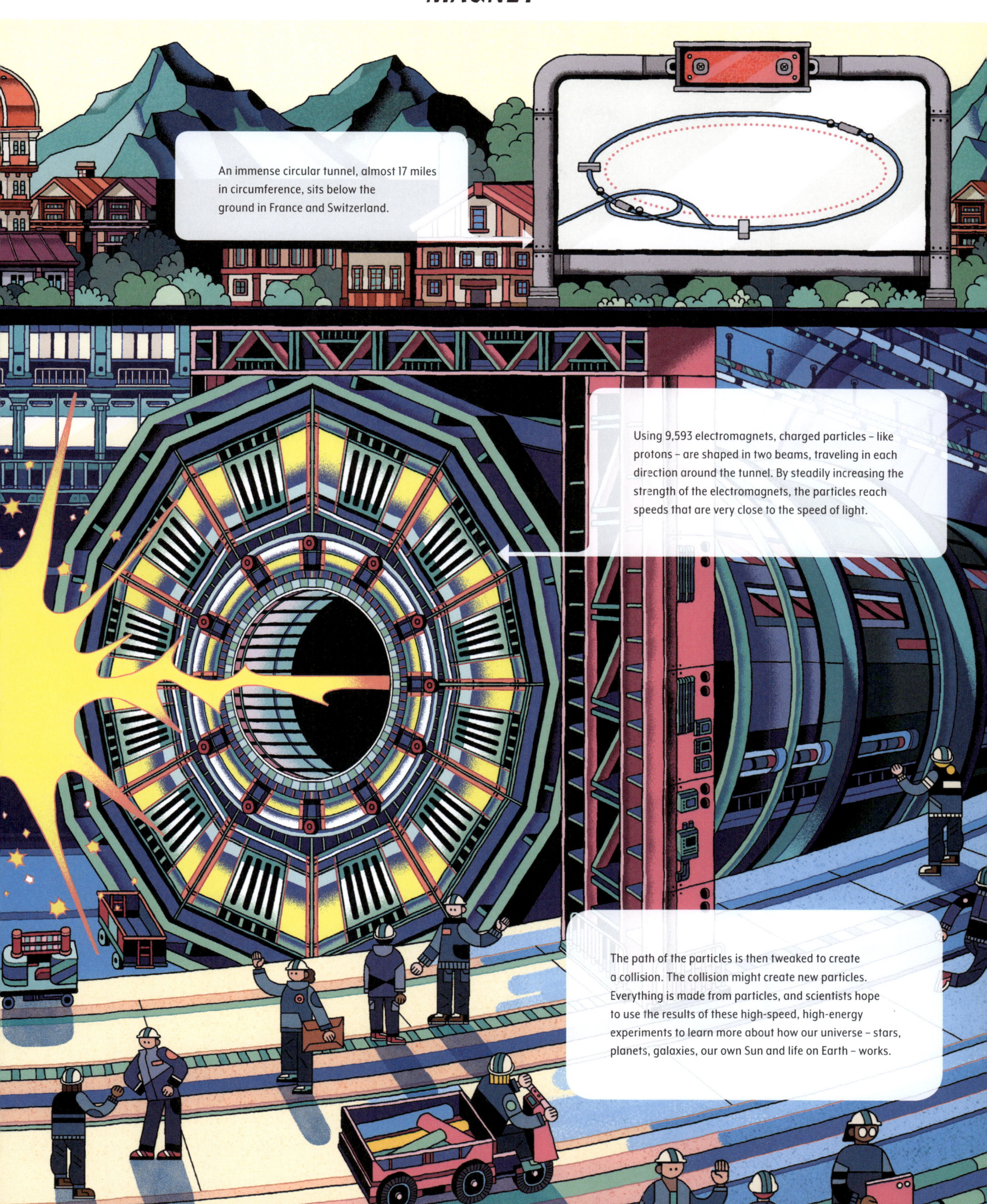

An immense circular tunnel, almost 17 miles in circumference, sits below the ground in France and Switzerland.

Using 9,593 electromagnets, charged particles – like protons – are shaped in two beams, traveling in each direction around the tunnel. By steadily increasing the strength of the electromagnets, the particles reach speeds that are very close to the speed of light.

The path of the particles is then tweaked to create a collision. The collision might create new particles. Everything is made from particles, and scientists hope to use the results of these high-speed, high-energy experiments to learn more about how our universe – stars, planets, galaxies, our own Sun and life on Earth – works.

THE LENS

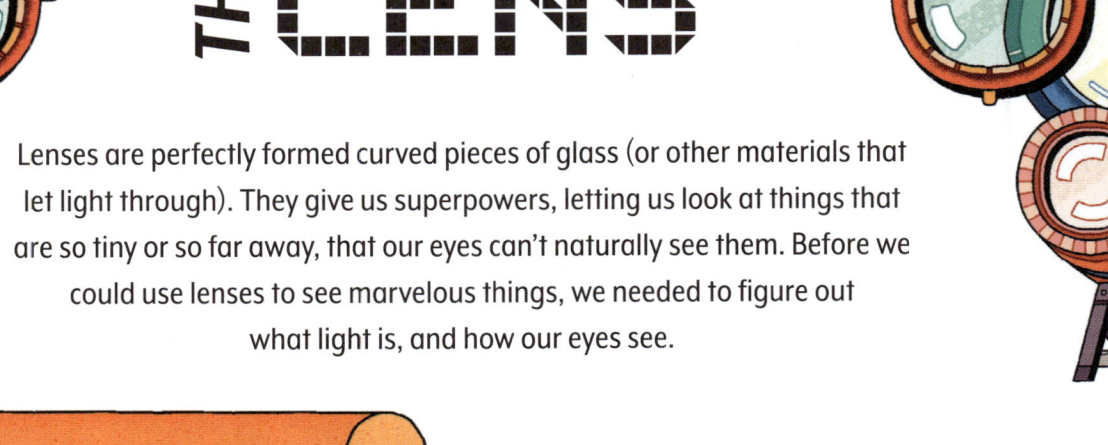

Lenses are perfectly formed curved pieces of glass (or other materials that let light through). They give us superpowers, letting us look at things that are so tiny or so far away, that our eyes can't naturally see them. Before we could use lenses to see marvelous things, we needed to figure out what light is, and how our eyes see.

In 965 CE, Ibn al-Haytham was born in Basra, in today's southern Iraq. He finally explained how our eyes work. He realized that light comes from sources such as the Sun, fire and lamps, and that this light bounces off objects around us into our eyes. Our eyes then send signals about the light to the brain, which creates images.

Also in the seventeenth century, telescopes using lenses were invented to show us objects in space that are very far away. Now we could see the craters on the Moon, the rings around Saturn, and even the Milky Way.

Around 700 years later, in the seventeenth century, microscopes were invented that used one or more lenses. Dutch inventor Antonie van Leeuwenhoek made microscopes with a single tiny lens, which was less than 0.03 in (inches) wide, to look at blood, pond water and different parts of the body. These were the first lenses to see red blood cells, algae and bacteria.

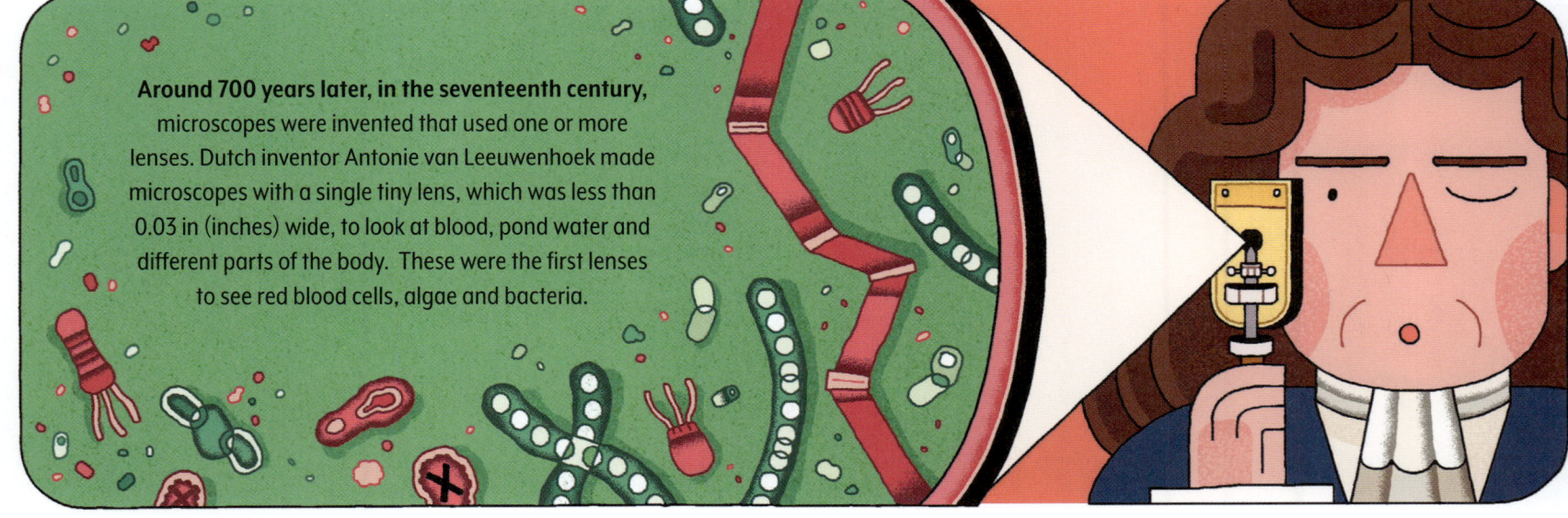

38

About 200 years later, Louis-Jacques-Mandé Daguerre invented the 'daguerreotype' camera, which used a lens in front of a 'film' – a sheet of copper coated with silver exposed to iodine vapor. To take a photograph of a person, they had to stand very still for up to half an hour, because it took a long time for the image of the person to imprint itself on to this film. These cameras were large and had dangerous chemicals. Over time, film and lens design became more sophisticated and cameras got smaller until photos could be taken by anyone in just a fraction of a second.

Frederick Douglass was an American former enslaved person and activist against slavery, who lived in the **nineteenth century**. He used photography to show the true humanity and diversity of black people in the United States.

In 1990, NASA and the European Space Agency sent the Hubble Space Telescope into space. Hubble has given us some of the most stunning images of stars and planets ever captured.

LENS

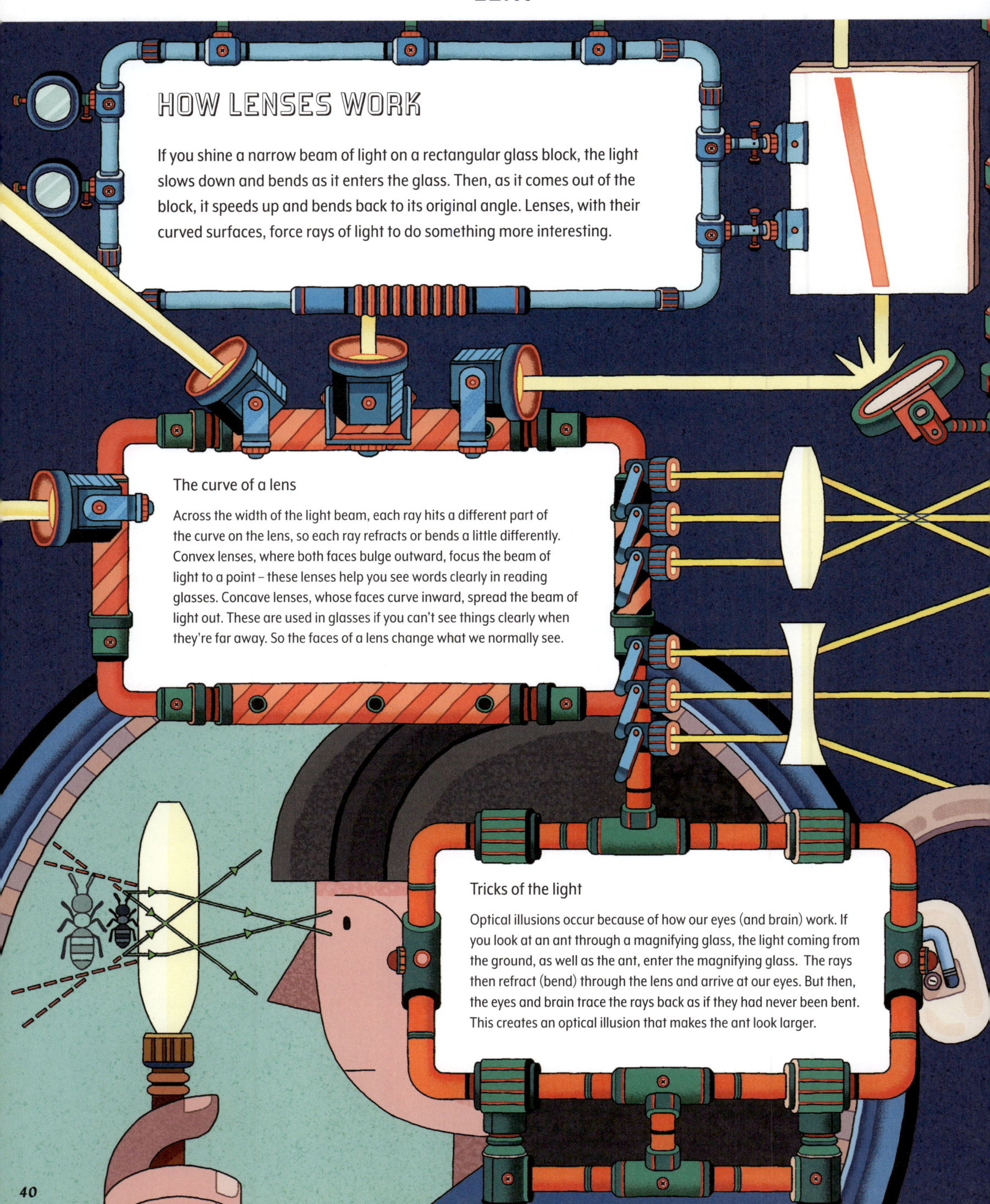

HOW LENSES WORK

If you shine a narrow beam of light on a rectangular glass block, the light slows down and bends as it enters the glass. Then, as it comes out of the block, it speeds up and bends back to its original angle. Lenses, with their curved surfaces, force rays of light to do something more interesting.

The curve of a lens

Across the width of the light beam, each ray hits a different part of the curve on the lens, so each ray refracts or bends a little differently. Convex lenses, where both faces bulge outward, focus the beam of light to a point – these lenses help you see words clearly in reading glasses. Concave lenses, whose faces curve inward, spread the beam of light out. These are used in glasses if you can't see things clearly when they're far away. So the faces of a lens change what we normally see.

Tricks of the light

Optical illusions occur because of how our eyes (and brain) work. If you look at an ant through a magnifying glass, the light coming from the ground, as well as the ant, enter the magnifying glass. The rays then refract (bend) through the lens and arrive at our eyes. But then, the eyes and brain trace the rays back as if they had never been bent. This creates an optical illusion that makes the ant look larger.

LENS

The sharpest lens

Light bends depending on its wavelength, so red light bends slightly differently to blue light. There are tiny differences in how the light bends when it is close to the center of the lens compared to when it is further out – these differences cause a phenomenon called 'aberration'. To solve this, scientists combine two lenses from different types of glass that cancel out aberrations and we get an even sharper picture.

Even transparent glass reflects some light, which might cause distracting reflections. In the 1930s, scientist Katharine Burr Blodgett invented an early antireflective layer, when she developed a coating for glass. Only a few molecules thick, this coating increased the amount of light traveling through the lens and stopped it reflecting. This science is now used to help people who wear glasses see more clearly.

LENS

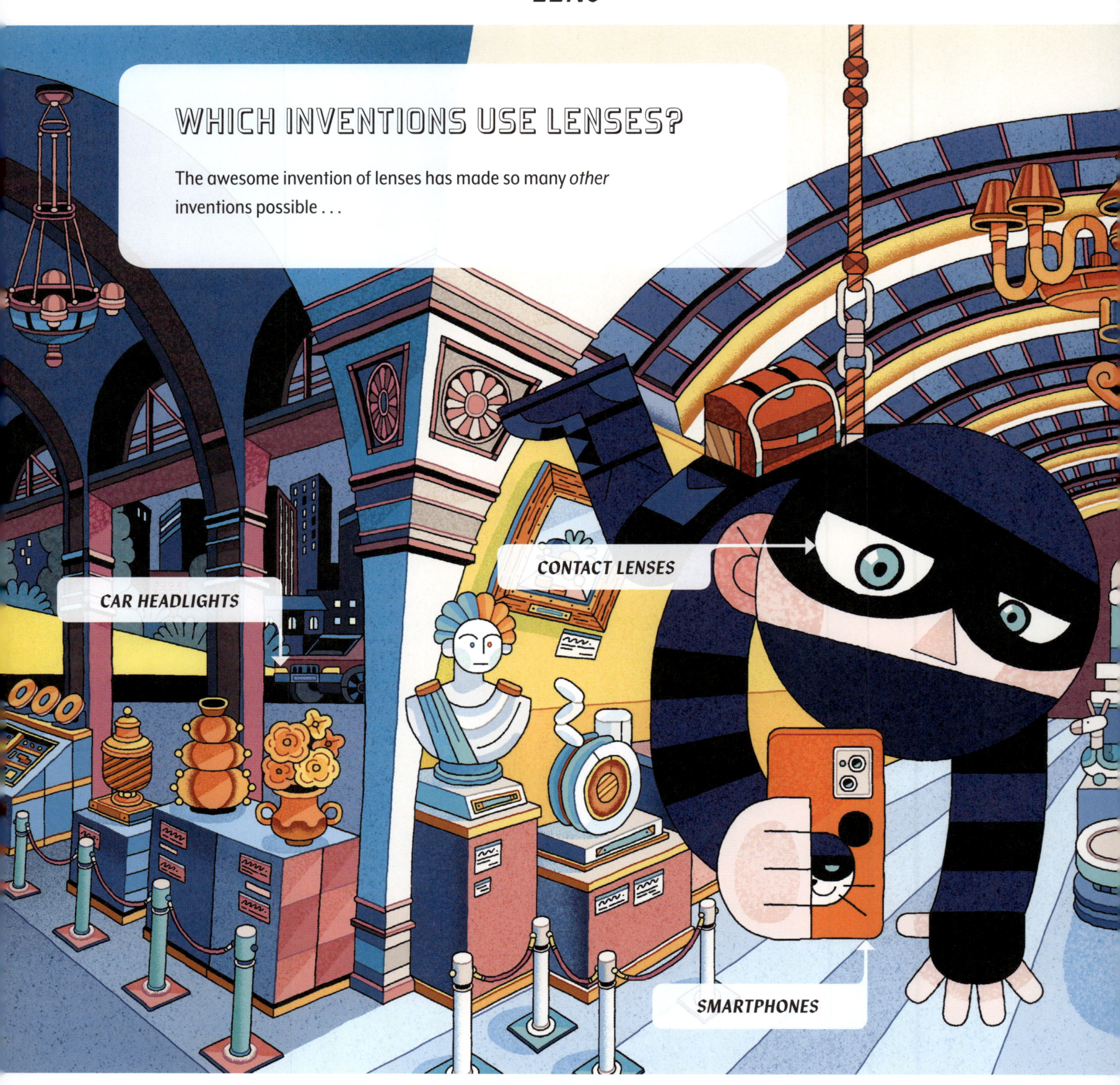

WHICH INVENTIONS USE LENSES?

The awesome invention of lenses has made so many *other* inventions possible . . .

CAR HEADLIGHTS

CONTACT LENSES

SMARTPHONES

CAR HEADLIGHTS
Lenses in front of a lamp spread the light out so other drivers can see the light without being dazzled by it.

CONTACT LENSES
Special plastics called hydrogels are used to make flexible lenses that we can put on our eyeballs. When they are made wet with a liquid, the material absorbs the moisture and softens, and when it dries out, it hardens.

SMARTPHONES
The cameras in our smartphones have tiny lenses that collect light and focus it on to a small sensor. This records the image and then shows it to us on our screens.

BINOCULARS
Binoculars help us see birds and animals that are far away. Light bends through a pair of lenses, but these turn the image upside down. Pyramid-shaped pieces of glass, called prisms, turn the image the right way up.

LENS

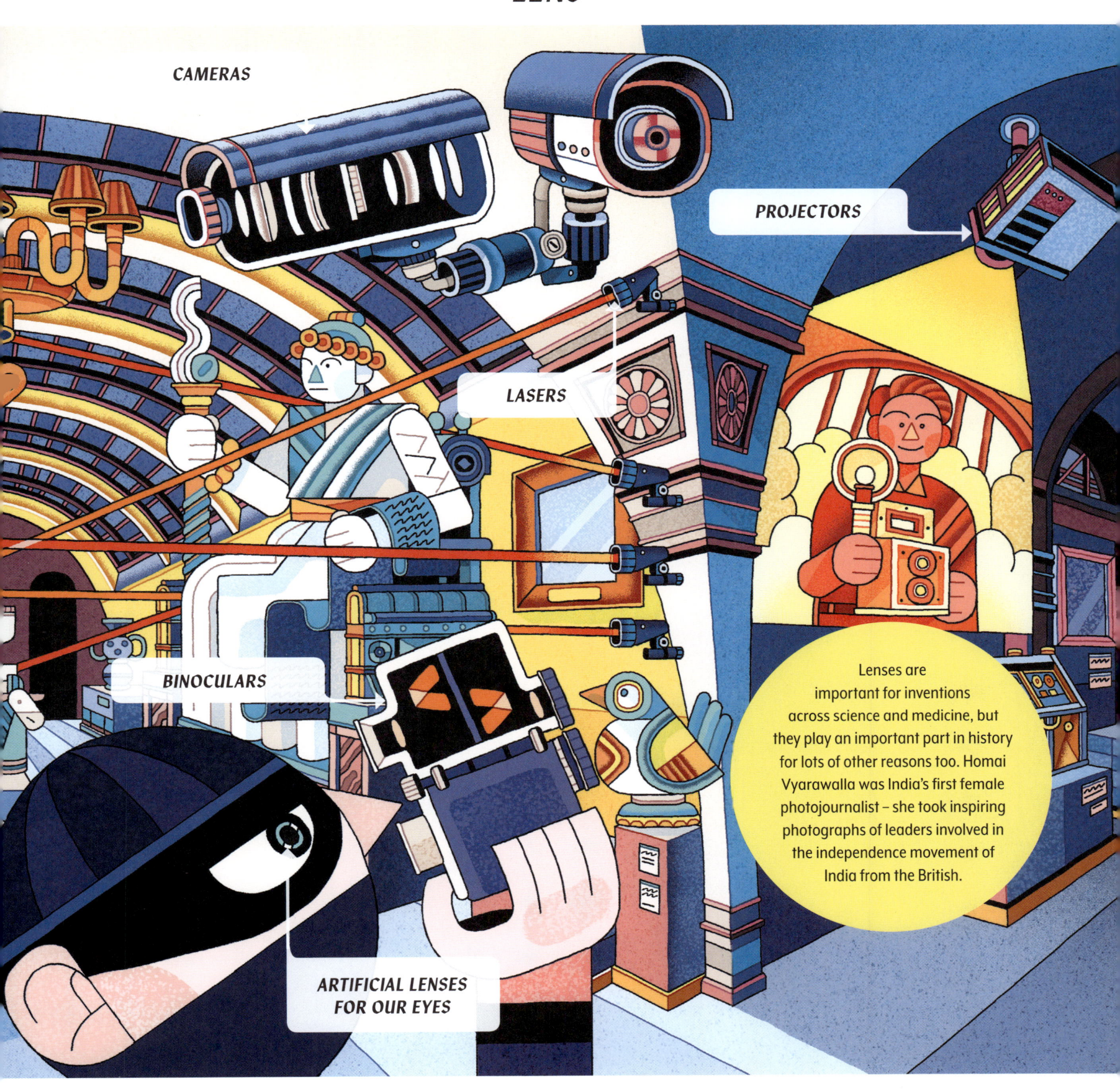

CAMERAS

PROJECTORS

LASERS

BINOCULARS

ARTIFICIAL LENSES FOR OUR EYES

Lenses are important for inventions across science and medicine, but they play an important part in history for lots of other reasons too. Homai Vyarawalla was India's first female photojournalist – she took inspiring photographs of leaders involved in the independence movement of India from the British.

CAMERAS
A camera often has different lenses that you can attach to its front to take close ups, or wide images, or zoom in on objects that are far away. But inside each of these 'lenses' are up to 12 individual lenses, which you can adjust to take the perfect picture!

ARTIFICIAL LENSES FOR OUR EYES
As we age, the natural lenses in our eyes can sometimes get cloudy. Tiny artificial lenses – called intraocular lenses – can replace a cloudy lens to help us see better.

LASERS
Laser beams are very narrow beams of a single color of light. Lenses are used to focus a laser beam down to a very sharp point, allowing it to cut materials such as diamonds, or even perform surgery.

PROJECTORS
These devices, used in schools, offices and movie theaters, use lenses to project a large image of a slide or movie on to a screen.

43

LENS

MICROSCOPES

Today's microscopes are incredibly powerful. Not only can they look at cells – the building blocks of all living things – but also inside cells. This means we can study viruses and bacteria, and create lifesaving medicines and vaccines.

Upright microscopes

These microscopes are ideal for looking at blood, pond water and the tiny organisms that live within them. You place your sample on a 'slide' – a very thin piece of glass – and then look at it through the eyepiece. Objects are magnified up to 2,000 times.

LENS

Electron microscopes (magnetic 'lens')

These are some of the most powerful microscopes around. They use beams of electrons to 'see' things, rather than light. They can magnify objects over *2 million* times! With these microscopes, you can see inside cells, admire the scales of an insect and even spot individual atoms in metals.

Inverted microscopes

In these microscopes, the lenses and light are arranged so that you look up at the sample. Instead of very thin samples fixed on a slide, you can place things like living cells in a liquid. The liquid creates a natural environment for the cells, and we can watch them while they are alive – that's how scientists discovered that cells divide.

STRING

String might not be the first thing you think of when asked about the greatest inventions of all time, but it's an incredible piece of engineering because it is strong *and* flexible at the same time.

Before we start, here are some useful words to understand:

FIBER
A thread-like part that can be made into cloth, including paper cloth.

THREAD
A fine strand of fiber used in sewing.

STRING
A twisted bundle of fibers. This is thicker than thread, and is sometimes made from two or more strands of thread twisted together.

YARN
Fiber, thread or string used in crafting to create cloth.

ROPE
Bundles of string that have been twisted or braided together to make it chunkier and stronger.

CABLE
A very strong, thick rope made from wires.

In nature, insects such as spiders and silkworms create strong threads, but the first time that humans made threads from the materials around us was an astonishing **40–50,000 years ago.** In a set of caves called the Abri du Maras in France, archaeologists found a stone tool that had a tiny piece of string on it, just 0.2 in long and 0.01 in thick. It was made from tree bark by our ancient cousins, the Neanderthals.

Around 100,000 years ago, humans first wore animal skins, bark and grass to cover their bodies, and they stitched these together with string. For the following tens of thousands of years, we continued to make string and rope from natural fibers, such as bark, animal hair, leaves and grass.

In around 6,000 BCE, humans were using linen that had been woven by string. We know this because archaeologists found a skeleton in Çatalhöyük in Anatolia (modern-day Turkey) wrapped in linen.

Then, **between 5,000 and 3,000 BCE,** Egyptians and Indians developed technology to spin linen and cotton quickly to create long, strong thread. We also learned to produce wool (another type of thread) from sheep. And we used different threads to make cloth made from natural fibers such as silk, wool, cotton and hemp, trading them along the Silk Road **for nearly 2,000 years.** We still use all these fibers in our clothes today!

In the late sixteenth century, the stocking frame and mechanical knitting machines were invented. And **over the next 200 years,** the production of cloth exploded in Europe and North America thanks to more machines such as the flying shuttle (to weave cloth) and the spinning jenny (which spun thread).

In the 1930s, we made the first ever artificial fiber (thread) called nylon from chemicals in a laboratory. It was used for stockings, parachutes, and ropes. Today, we have a huge range of artificial fibers, such as polyester, acrylic, modal and spandex.

STRING

HOW STRING WORKS

String is made from fibers or small thin threads. A single fiber on its own is fragile and not particularly useful, so, to make it stronger, several fibers need to be combined. The fibers rub up against each other and the frictional forces between them are what gives the string strength.

Twisting string

The Neanderthal string we found in French caves was made from twisted fibers extracted from bark. The direction of the twist is known as an 'S-twist' because, like the middle section of the letter S, you can see the fibres wrapping from the top left to the bottom right along the length of the yarn. Then, three separate pieces of yarn were twisted to form cord in the opposite direction – known as a Z-twist.

Layering fibers

If you twisted your fibers to create yarn in one direction, and then twisted multiple pieces of yarn in the same direction to strengthen it, you would fail because a small tug would cause the twists to unwind and the string to stretch out and unravel. So layers need to be twisted in opposite directions.

STRING

Natural fiber

Our most important natural fiber today, wool, is built up from lots of complicated layers of keratin (a protein that also makes up our nails and hair). If you looked at wool under a very strong microscope, you'd be able to see parts of it twisted together in opposite directions, just like how we make yarn.

Artificial fiber

Scientists can invent new artificial fibers that are even stronger and are made from chemicals. A chemist called Stephanie Kwolek experimented with long chains of molecules called polymers to make a strong fiber to use in the tires of racing cars. From this experience she invented Kevlar, a fibre that is now also used in sports clothing, tennis racket strings, car brakes, bridge cables and firefighting equipment.

Musical strings

Strings are great for music because all sound comes from vibrations. If you tie a string tightly at each end and pluck it, it vibrates and produces a sound. Depending on how heavy and thick the string is, and the distance between the fixed ends, you can create different notes. You need a strong and flexible material for this!

STRING

WHICH INVENTIONS USE STRING?

Thanks to the invention of string, all these inventions are possible...

- SITARS
- GUITARS
- TAMBOURA
- VIOLINS

TAMBOURA
The tamboura isn't used to play tunes. Instead, its four metal strings are plucked in sequence to create a droning sound that forms the background for other instruments. There are also short cotton threads – called jiva – towards the base of the four metal strings that help tune them.

GUITARS
Guitars have six strings: three are typically simple lengths of wire, while the other three are called 'wrapped' strings. These have a single wire with another long wire wrapped around it to create heavier strings for lower notes. Guitar strings are usually made from metal or nylon, an artificial fiber.

VIOLINS
Although violin strings are usually now made from artificial materials, they used to be made from lamb's guts! Collagen, a substance found in skin, ligaments and tendons, is collected from lamb's intestines and soaked in a series of chemicals. Once cleaned, the fibers are stretched, twisted and dried under tension.

SITARS
Sitars usually have 18 to 21 strings. Five to seven of these are the main strings, which create the melody, while the rest are called 'sympathetic' strings. When the main strings are played, they cause the others to vibrate and create a lingering sound.

STRING

Q'ESWACHAKA BRIDGE

COLORED FABRICS

CLOTHES

MASKS

COLORED FABRICS
A couple of hundred years ago, pink was more often used for boys' clothes. It was considered a shade of the military color red. Girls more often wore blue, the color worn by the Virgin Mary.

CLOTHES
Our earliest clothes were made from animal skins, but then we switched to cloth woven from string, which is what we still use today.

Q'ESWACHAKA BRIDGE IN PERU
This handwoven rope bridge, made by the Inca people, proves that twisted rope makes a great structural material when pulled or put in tension. Since rope is made from many fibers, it won't fail without warning even if some of the fibers stretch and snap.

MASKS
Medical or surgical masks, such as those used during the Covid pandemic, are made from a random arrangement of fibers, like spaghetti on a plate. The randomness makes the material much better at catching small particles, such as viruses.

STRING

RAJIV GANDHI SEALINK

The Rajiv Gandhi Sealink in Mumbai, India, is an enormous eight-lane road bridge that crosses a bay in the Arabian Sea. Just like yarn, steel wires can also be bundled together to create cables, which are incredibly strong and are used in some of the biggest bridges around the world.

The Rajiv Gandhi Sealink is India's first cable-stayed bridge over a sea.

A large section of the bridge is supported by cables, which creates clear areas for fishing boats to sail under.

The total length of cables used was 1,398 miles (mi), and they support 22,046 tons (t) of weight – the equivalent of 3,000 African elephants!

STRING

The cables are made from steel wires that are 0.27 in across. Between 60 to 120 of these wires were laid in parallel in a factory to create each of the cables.

The cables fan out from tall pylons or columns that are tied to the seabed.

A cable with 60 wires can support the weight of a blue whale!

THE PUMP

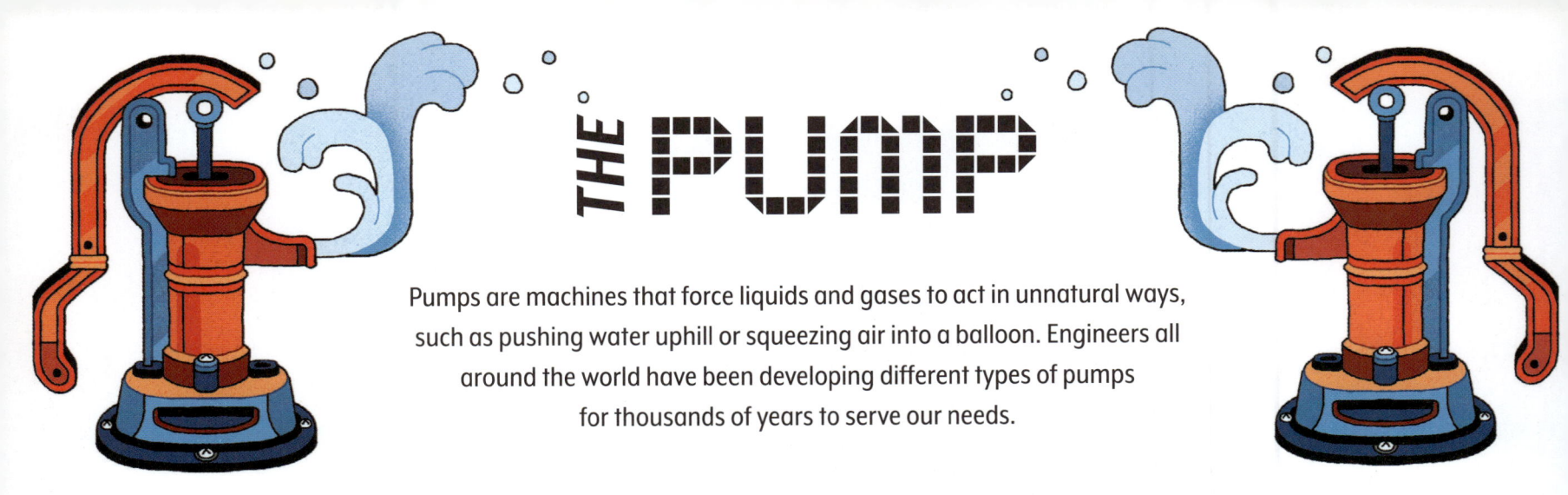

Pumps are machines that force liquids and gases to act in unnatural ways, such as pushing water uphill or squeezing air into a balloon. Engineers all around the world have been developing different types of pumps for thousands of years to serve our needs.

Around 5,000 years ago, in ancient Mesopotamia (modern-day Iraq), the people who lived there needed to transport water to grow crops. They used the shadoof, which looked like a seesaw with a very tall support. Sitting on top of a frame, the shadoof's long pole had a bucket attached to one end and a counterweight to the other. This allowed people to raise water up from the rivers and distribute it to land.

In around 300 BCE, the ancient Egyptians had a similar problem of how to transport water, and used a hollow wooden tube with a long screw-like cylinder inside. One end was dipped into a river or lake, and the other was higher up on land. As you twisted the screw, the threads trapped water inside the tube and the water was pulled up. This method is still used by farmers along the River Nile in Egypt today.

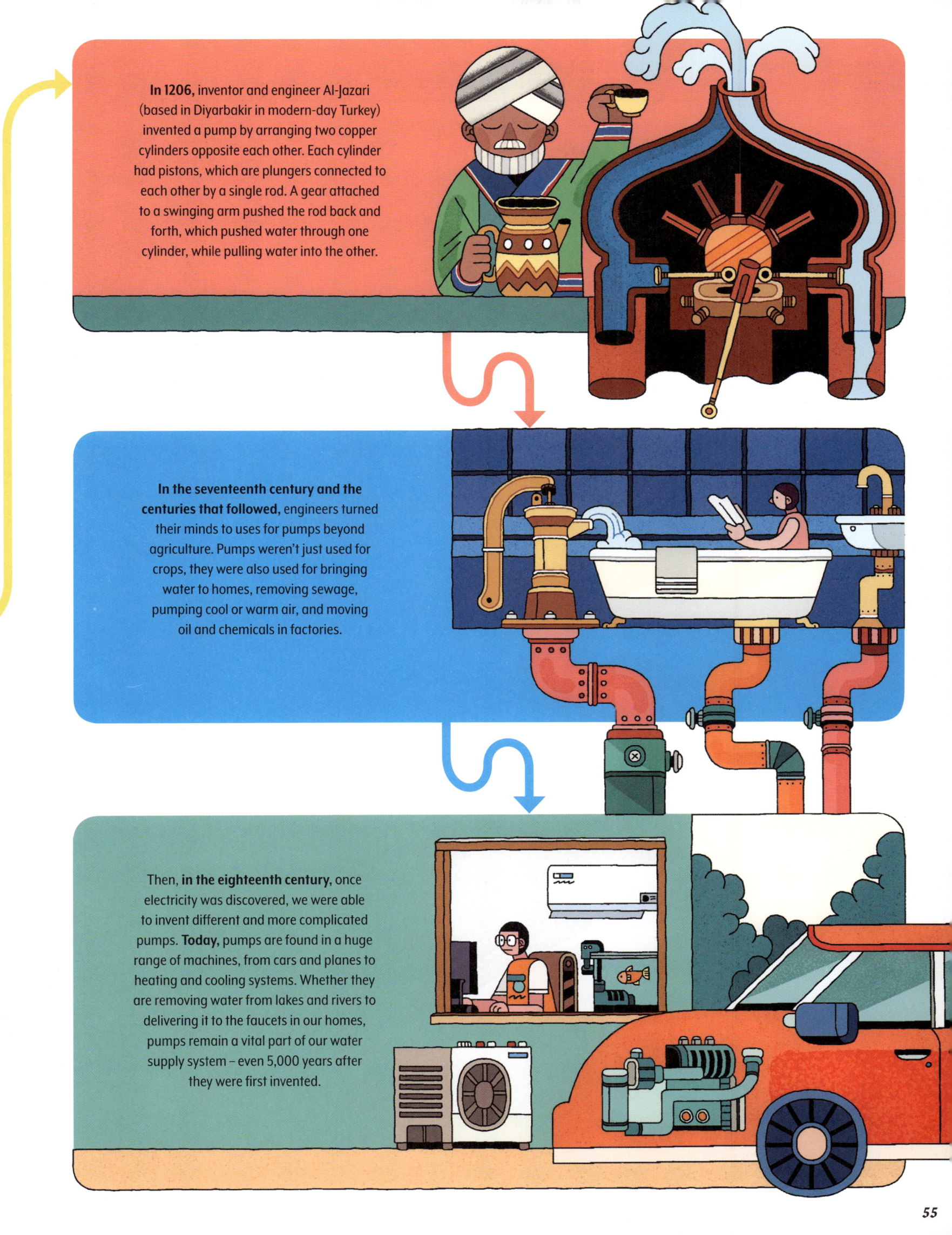

In 1206, inventor and engineer Al-Jazari (based in Diyarbakir in modern-day Turkey) invented a pump by arranging two copper cylinders opposite each other. Each cylinder had pistons, which are plungers connected to each other by a single rod. A gear attached to a swinging arm pushed the rod back and forth, which pushed water through one cylinder, while pulling water into the other.

In the seventeenth century and the centuries that followed, engineers turned their minds to uses for pumps beyond agriculture. Pumps weren't just used for crops, they were also used for bringing water to homes, removing sewage, pumping cool or warm air, and moving oil and chemicals in factories.

Then, **in the eighteenth century,** once electricity was discovered, we were able to invent different and more complicated pumps. **Today,** pumps are found in a huge range of machines, from cars and planes to heating and cooling systems. Whether they are removing water from lakes and rivers to delivering it to the faucets in our homes, pumps remain a vital part of our water supply system – even 5,000 years after they were first invented.

PUMP

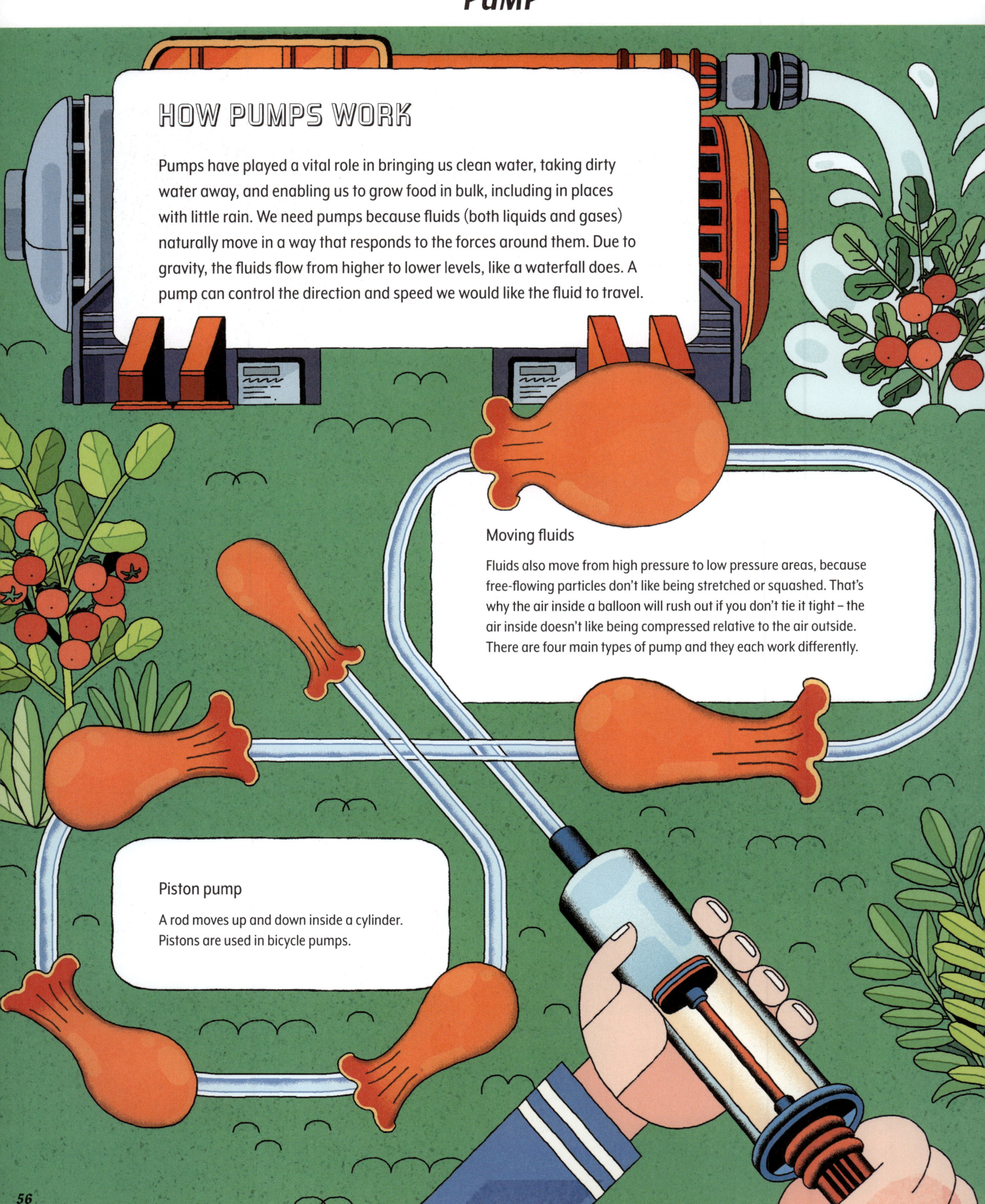

HOW PUMPS WORK

Pumps have played a vital role in bringing us clean water, taking dirty water away, and enabling us to grow food in bulk, including in places with little rain. We need pumps because fluids (both liquids and gases) naturally move in a way that responds to the forces around them. Due to gravity, the fluids flow from higher to lower levels, like a waterfall does. A pump can control the direction and speed we would like the fluid to travel.

Moving fluids

Fluids also move from high pressure to low pressure areas, because free-flowing particles don't like being stretched or squashed. That's why the air inside a balloon will rush out if you don't tie it tight – the air inside doesn't like being compressed relative to the air outside. There are four main types of pump and they each work differently.

Piston pump

A rod moves up and down inside a cylinder. Pistons are used in bicycle pumps.

PUMP

Rotary pump
These have rotating wheels or gears. Rotary pumps are used to move oil in machines.

Centrifugal pump
A part of the pump spins rapidly and pushes fluid outwards until the fluid hits a pipe and is released. Centrifugal pumps are used in lawn sprinklers.

Diaphragm pump
A flexible membrane is controlled by a source of power that vibrates back and forth. Diaphragm pumps are used to move sewage and oil.

PUMP

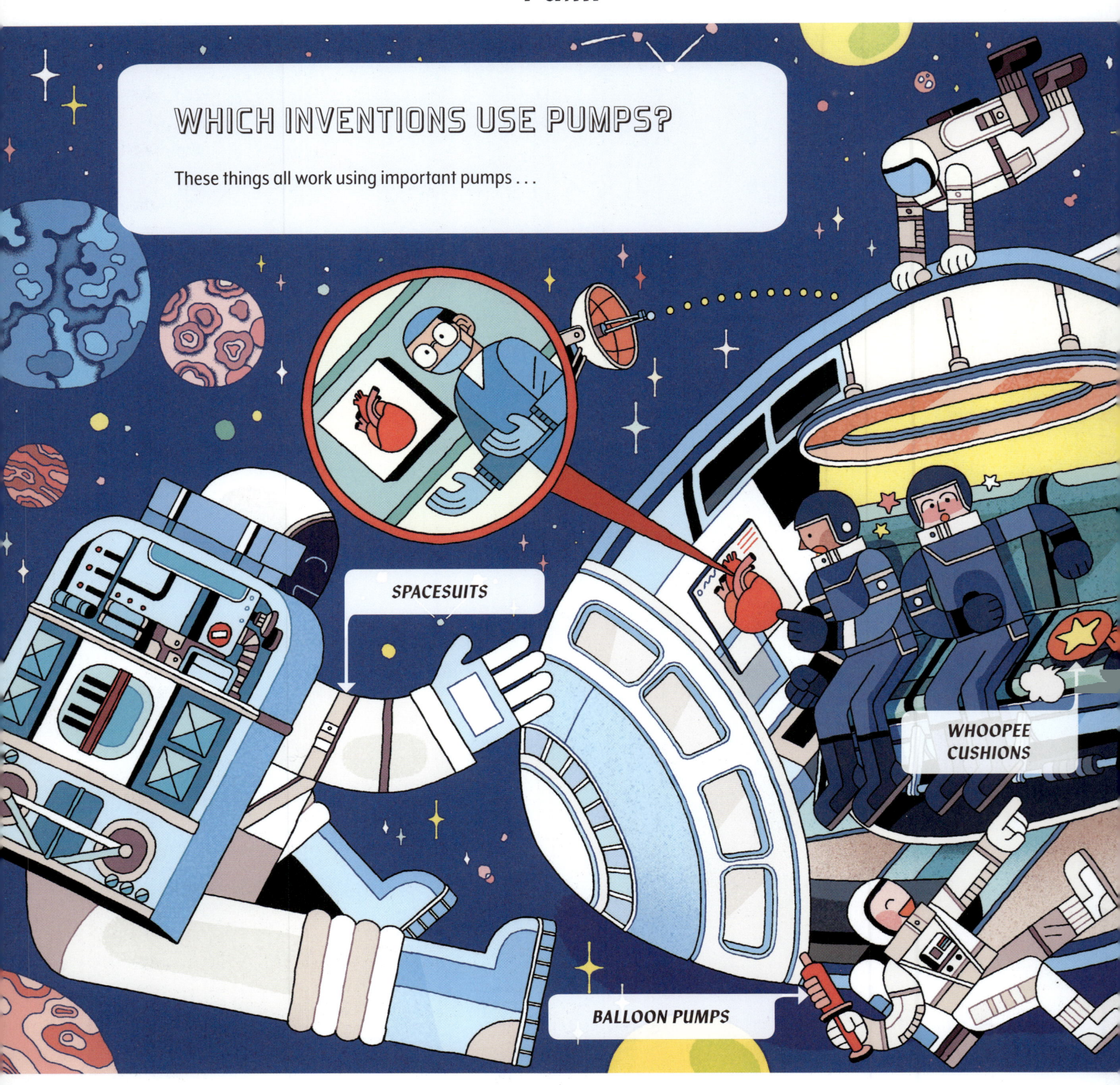

WHICH INVENTIONS USE PUMPS?

These things all work using important pumps...

SPACESUITS

BALLOON PUMPS

WHOOPEE CUSHIONS

SPACESUITS
Pumps have helped humans go to space! To help the astronaut breathe, one pump takes oxygen into the inside layer of their spacesuit and helmet, while another pump keeps the astronaut cool.

BALLOON PUMPS
These great little piston pumps help us fill balloons with air, rather than using our lungs, which get tired after a while!

WHOOPEE CUSHIONS
Whoopee cushions create farty noises by pushing air out through a small flap, and as the air rushes out, the flap opens and shuts, making funny sounds! They have been used for thousands of years!

PUMP

THRUSTER ENGINES

HEART-LUNG MACHINES

HEARTS

THRUSTER ENGINES
Spacecraft often have engines called thrusters that help them navigate. These can use waste water or gases produced in the spacecraft, which are stored at a high pressure. A switch pushes these fluids out, which gush out at speed, and power the engine.

HEARTS
Not technically an invention by humans, but our hearts are still amazing! They beat around 100,000 times a day. Hearts are pumps made from muscles that circulate blood around our lungs to absorb oxygen; then they take this blood to deliver oxygen to the rest of our bodies.

HEART-LUNG MACHINES
John and Mary Gibbon created the heart-lung machine, an artificial heart-and-lung system that humans can be hooked up to. A rotary pump gently pumps blood around the body instead of the heart, so the heart can be stopped and operated on.

PUMP

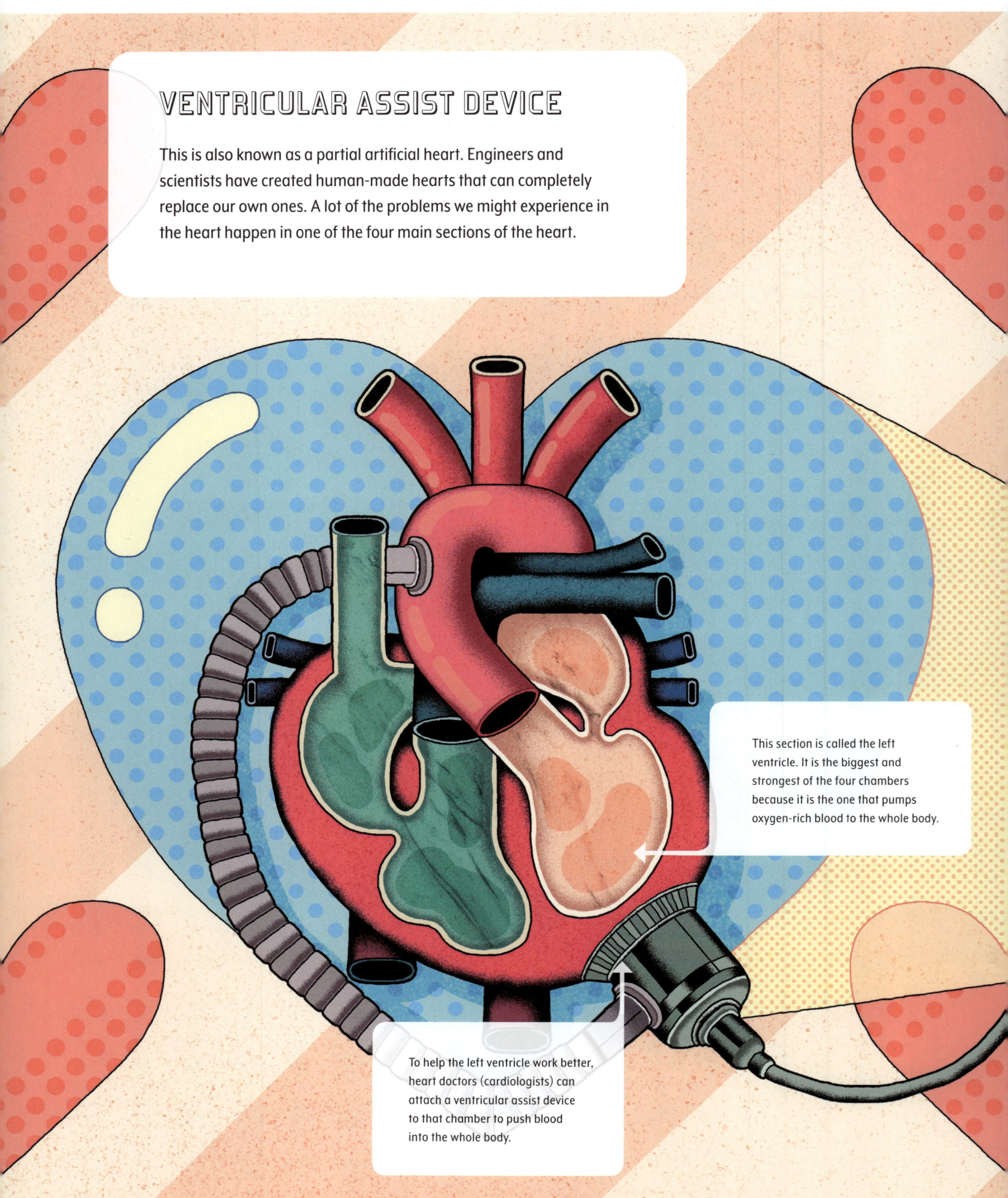

VENTRICULAR ASSIST DEVICE

This is also known as a partial artificial heart. Engineers and scientists have created human-made hearts that can completely replace our own ones. A lot of the problems we might experience in the heart happen in one of the four main sections of the heart.

This section is called the left ventricle. It is the biggest and strongest of the four chambers because it is the one that pumps oxygen-rich blood to the whole body.

To help the left ventricle work better, heart doctors (cardiologists) can attach a ventricular assist device to that chamber to push blood into the whole body.

PUMP

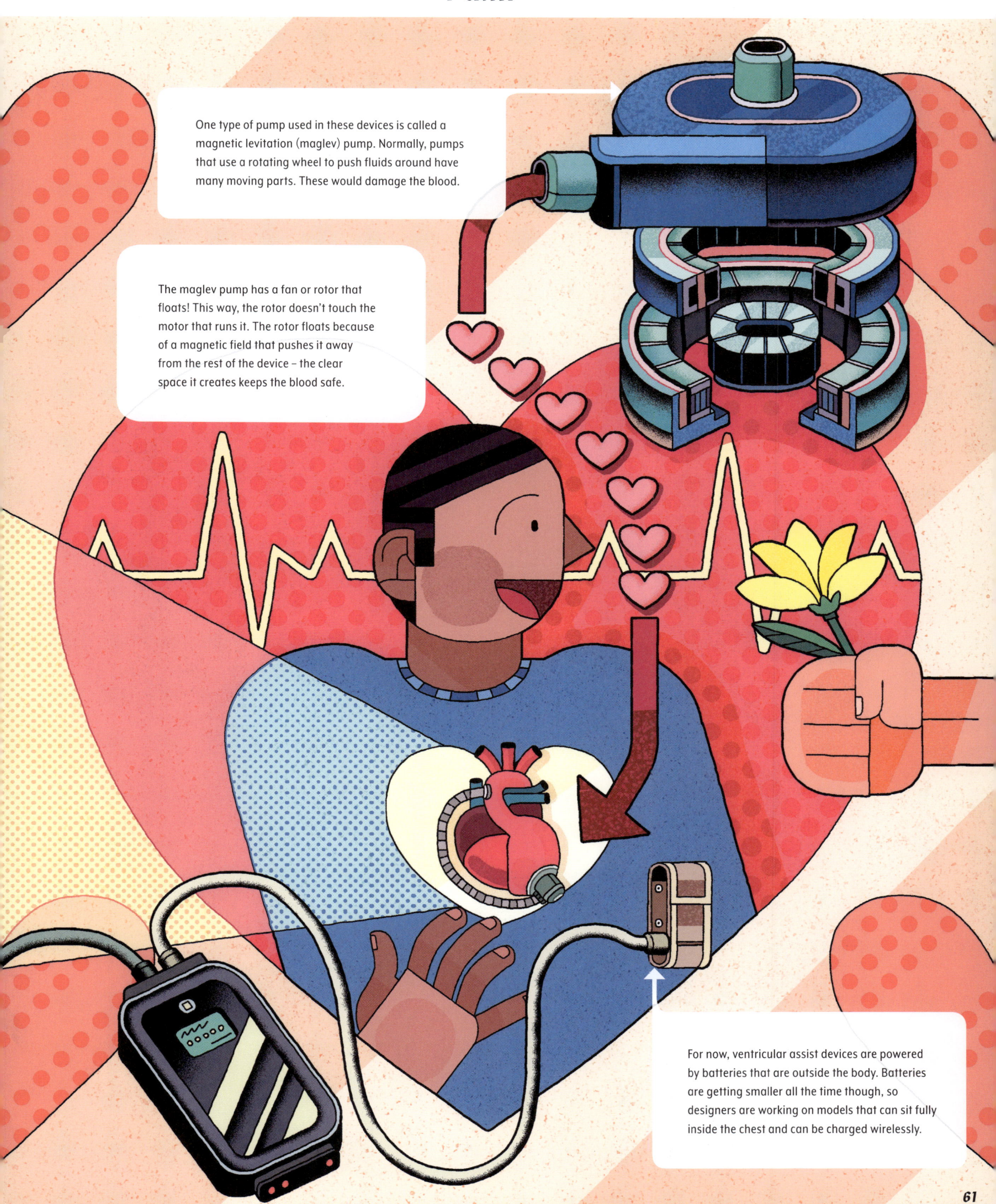

One type of pump used in these devices is called a magnetic levitation (maglev) pump. Normally, pumps that use a rotating wheel to push fluids around have many moving parts. These would damage the blood.

The maglev pump has a fan or rotor that floats! This way, the rotor doesn't touch the motor that runs it. The rotor floats because of a magnetic field that pushes it away from the rest of the device – the clear space it creates keeps the blood safe.

For now, ventricular assist devices are powered by batteries that are outside the body. Batteries are getting smaller all the time though, so designers are working on models that can sit fully inside the chest and can be charged wirelessly.

WHAT WILL YOU INVENT?

The technology and engineering that surrounds us every day can seem really complicated and intimidating – how are you supposed to understand how they work, let alone try to invent anything yourself?! Well, my best advice is to . . .

. . . get curious!

Now that you've discovered the amazing stories behind the seven objects in this book, get out there and be curious about other stuff you see around you. You can ask yourself: when was it first invented? By whom? What is it – or was it – made from? How did its design change over the years? Who are the amazing people involved in its invention and evolution?

And the most important question to ask is . . .

How can we do it better?

Our engineering and technology has a big impact on us and our planet. Being on our screens and phones so much causes stress, and we go outside less. We mine precious minerals from the Earth, emit carbon and chemicals as waste while making stuff, and after we use something for a little while, we throw it away.

On average, in the UK, every person gets rid of almost 53 lbs of electronics each year. The clothing and textile industry creates over 101 million t of waste globally each year.

By understanding the world around us better, asking questions, and seeking answers, we can make smarter choices about what we buy and use. To help us live happily, and to also help the planet.

So, before you just throw stuff away . . .

* Ask an adult's permission first!

Stop. Think. Question. Reuse. And if you can (and it's safe to do so*) . . .

. . . repair! Breaking things apart to see how they're made is one of the best ways to understand the human-made objects around us. In trying to fix it, you might just make amazing discoveries and inventions of your own.

What will YOU find out?